Bound by Consent
Copyright©2013 Dalia Craig
ISBN 978-1-909934-00-9
Cover art and design by Dalia

Published by
Lydian Press 2013
Find us on the World Wide Web at
www.lydianpress.com

Contents:

All the above titles were originally published as individual eBooks by loveyoudivine Alterotica

Foreword:

Bound By Consent contains five short stories charting about a year in the lives of two women, Bryana Austin and Cassie Stuart, following them from a chance encounter on a Scottish mountain to London, Amsterdam, New York and finally back to Scotland.

Way back in 2008, when I embarked on Taming Bryana, the first story in this collection, I never intended it to be more than a single short story. Then several people said they wanted to know more about Bryana and Cassie and what happened to them.

In response, I began Slave to Lust, expanding on the lives of these two women by having them meet up again 6 months after Taming Bryana finished. However, that second story, left a few loose ends and unresolved issues. So I wrote another, Night Games, and then another, Meeting of Minds, both of these from Cassie's point of view. Finally, I wrote Full Circle, to bring Bryana and Cassie's story to an end. Or is it just the beginning?

Dalia Craig
September 2012

Dedication:

Larkin... *This book would never have been possible without your support. I love you to bits. Muah!*

Claudia... *Thank you for believing in me.*

Bound by Consent

Dalia Craig

From Scotland to London, Amsterdam, and New York, two women struggle to build an enduring relationship in the face of adversity.

Taming Bryana

Bryana

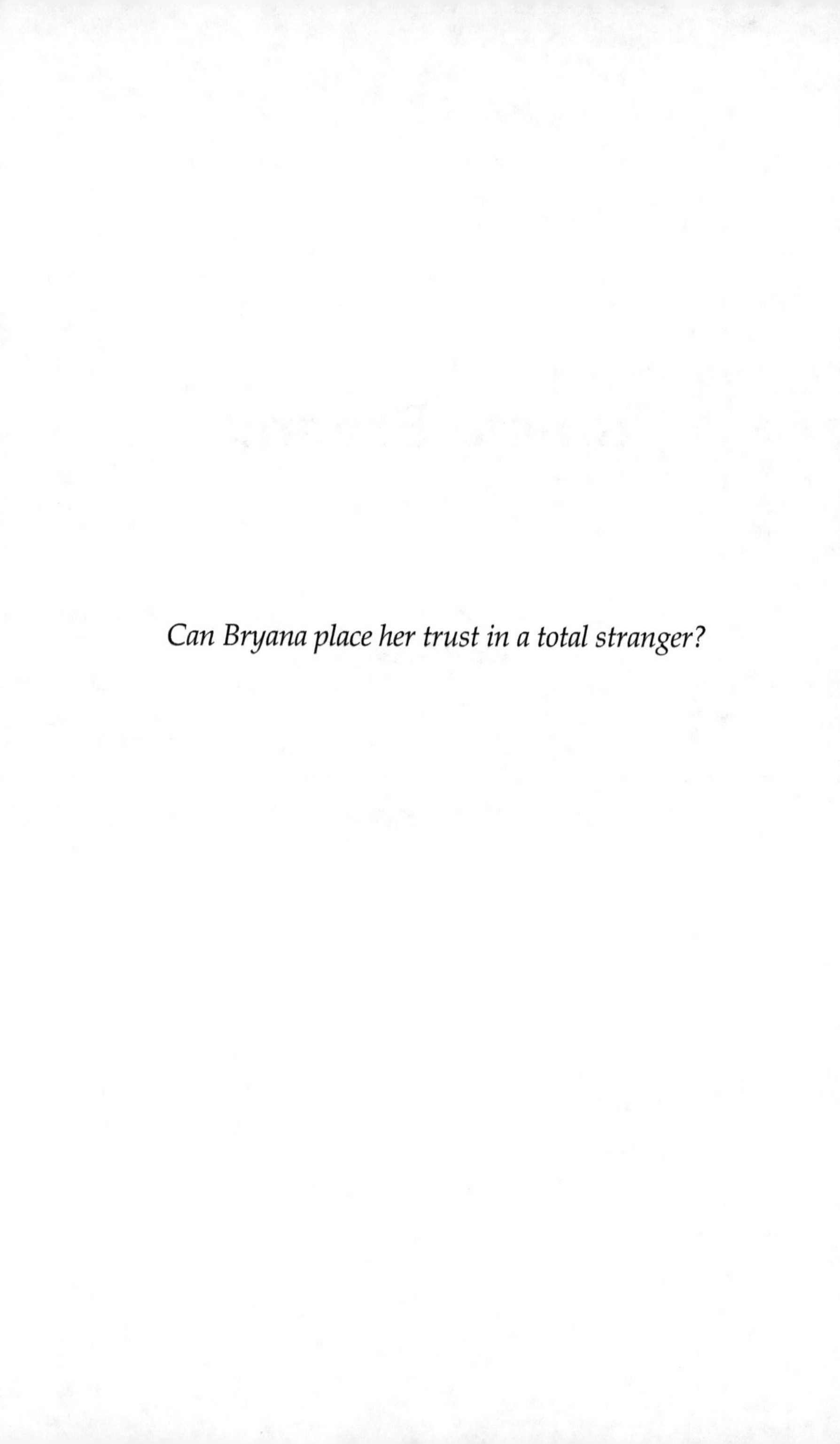

Can Bryana place her trust in a total stranger?

"You expect me to get up on *that*?"

I eyed the horse and wrinkled my nose with distaste at the unpleasant odor emanating from the stained gray blanket covering its back before switching my gaze to the butch dyke who'd ridden to my rescue. She had appeared out of the mist, mounted on an enormous, dark brown beast with evil eyes, with the other horse on a leading rein behind.

The woman, who'd introduced herself as Cassie Stuart, sat astride her mount with the easy confidence of someone who shared a close affinity with horses. With cropped dark hair and androgynous clothing, I had almost mistaken her for a man. Only the soft lilt of her voice betrayed her sex.

"It's your choice, Ms. Austin." Cassie glanced down to my feet then shrugged. "You either ride Tavish or face a five-mile walk to Auchtercairn."

Some choice.

My day had started badly and then rapidly nose dived into a total disaster leaving me at a loss to understand how I'd ended up in this predicament. One minute I was driving along a discernible mountain road in early evening sunshine and the next... Nothing. Both the view and the road had suddenly disappeared, obscured by a blanket of white mist. I hit the brakes, expecting the car to slow and eventually stop but nothing of the sort happened. Instead, Jazzy skidded off the road, gathering speed until it felt like she was flying, before eventually coming to a rest buried up to her axles in a sticky gooey mess of water and mud. I had no idea what damage had been done or how I was going to get her out and back on the road.

I shivered as the mist swirled around us. Although barely evening and still daylight, it might easily have been the middle of the night for all I could see. I momentarily regretted abandoning my shoes to the peat bog, but Jimmy Choo's were never designed for a five-mile hike in rough terrain and neither were stocking-clad feet. If I wanted the promised hot bath, some food, and a bed for the night, I'd have to grit my teeth and do it. I nodded agreement and edged closer to the fetid beast, my sense of unreality growing with every step.

How the hell does one mount something this tall without a ladder, especially dressed as I am in a tight skirt?

"Let me help you up, Bryana." Before I had the opportunity to protest that I'd changed my mind, Cassie freed her feet from the stirrups and sprang from her horse in one graceful movement. Then, in the blink of an eye, she had manipulated me into a position where, with no apparent effort, she hoisted me onto the horse.

Without a saddle or stirrups, I was forced to wrap my legs around Tavish and hang onto his long, silky mane as Cassie led the way along the narrow mountain track. But worse was to come when the friction of the rough horse blanket against my crotch began to drive me toward a climax.

God! What is the matter with me?

Sex should be the last thing on my mind right now; yet the memory of Cassie's strong hands gliding up my thighs, as she eased the pencil skirt up to enable me to sit astride Tavish, made me crave the satisfaction of a good hard fuck even more than the hot bath.

I prayed for a speedy end to this torment and forced myself to think of anything other than sex in the struggle to hang on to my sanity.

Whatever possessed me to accept a commission so far from civilization?

Why didn't I insist that we do the photo shoot for Esmée's new collection of designer tartan in my London studio rather than on some wild headland in the north of Scotland?

And, more importantly, why didn't I have the sense to stay put at the hotel until morning, like the rest of the crew, instead of driving off in a rage when I discovered Esmée fucking the brains out of that stuck-up bitch Marisa in our hotel bedroom?

God! I must have been blind not to see what was happening right under my nose. Now I know why Esmée always insisted on Marisa as her model of choice. Though what she saw in that haughty stick insect, I couldn't fathom and quite frankly didn't care; they were welcome to each other.

What I did care about was that Jazzy, my much loved Jaguar XJS convertible, together with all my valuable photographic equipment, was now stuck fast in a peat bog at the back end of nowhere, leaving me no option but to perch on this disgusting, smelly animal en route to some God-forsaken hovel.

Auchtercairn, when it finally loomed out of the swirling mist, disproved one misconception – it was as far removed from a hovel as one could get. Several security lights, switched on automatically by our approach, revealed a large square tower that dwarfed the well-preserved, gray-stone castle. The whole edifice sat squarely upon an outcrop of rugged cliffs above the sea. Cassie stopped at a side door, hitched the horses to a bar set into the stonework, helped me to dismount, and ushered me inside.

A bevy of dogs rushed to greet us with a flurry of wagging tails and excited barks.

"Don't mind them; they don't bite," Cassie shouted to be heard above the commotion; then, barely pausing to pet the furry heads, she crossed the stone-flagged hall in a few long strides and was halfway up the wide staircase before she glanced back and beckoned. "The bathroom's up here."

I followed in her wake, admiring the swing of her firm ass. Although I would never be caught dead wearing a thick plaid shirt or worn jeans tucked into long leather boots, I had to admit they looked incredibly sexy on her.

Once we reached the landing, Cassie opened a studded wooden door then stood aside to allow me to enter. "Help yourself to whatever you need; there's an assortment of bath oils to choose from, limitless hot water, and fresh towels in the press. Take as long as you want. I'll need to see to the horses and then get Hamish to tow your car in before I fix us some drinks and a meal." She paused; a frown creasing her brow as her gaze swept over my crumpled Giovanni d'Marco suit. "I'd better find you something more suitable to wear, too."

"Thank you." The door shut with a solid clunk almost before I'd spoken. I turned eagerly toward the claw-foot bath that dominated the center of the bathroom, my brain already dwelling on the luxury of soaking in hot water. That was before I glanced down at the muck still caked to my legs and feet. Yuck! I looked and smelt like a creature from the swamp, as though I'd stepped out of some horror film. No, I shook my head, I couldn't bear to soil that pristine white enamel. It would have to be a shower instead.

Twenty minutes later, I felt human again – clean, smelling of delicate white jasmine, a large towel wrapped sarong fashion around my breasts, and my long hair knotted at the nape of my neck. I explored the large room which was divided by a high partition. One side was fitted out as a luxury bathroom, and the other side furnished with an extensive range of fitness equipment reflected in a mirrored wall.

I shivered despite the warmth coming from the radiators; something about the modernity of all this hi-tech equipment didn't fit in with a late-seventeenth-century castle. On closer inspection, I saw that the mirrored wall was, in fact, a pair of sliding doors.

Do they lead to another room?

I knew it was none of my business to go poking around somebody's private domain but the temptation to take a peek behind the mirror was overwhelming. I felt a bit like *Alice in Wonderland* faced with a button that read "push me." I took a deep breath, placed one finger on the button, and the doors immediately slid apart with no more than a whisper.

Certain I was dreaming or had fallen down the proverbial rabbit hole, I stepped into a fantasy world: a windowless room with a vaulted ceiling which, I guessed by the roughness of the gray-stone walls, must form part of the tower. In the light from electric candles that flickered almost as eerily as the real thing, I drooled over the array of restraints which hung from the walls, each separated by filmy, red-silk drapes. A spanking stool and a swing stood ready for use in the middle of the room, a St. Andrews Cross set into an alcove to one side, and, the *pièce de résistance*, a black wrought-iron, four-poster bed dressed in red and black silk on a dais at the far end.

Oh joy! I could hardly believe my luck stumbling into this pleasure palace. My insides clenched as my imagination ran riot with various erotic scenarios; with the right mistress to exact punishment, this discovery could lead to a whole lot of fun.

Hold it. The sensible part of my brain took over. Tempering my excitement with some pertinent questions.

What is all this stuff doing in a remote Scottish castle?

Who apart from Cassie Stuart lives and plays here?

I fingered one of the spaghetti-string floggers lined up on the table with a host of whips, masks, and other…

"Ah, I see you discovered my playroom."

Fuck!

Heat crawled across my cheeks at being caught in the act. I spun around clashing with Cassie's sensual gaze. My heart fluttered in my chest as I took in the disarmingly sexy woman lounging casually against the doorframe. Although she still wore her jeans and those knee-length black and tan boots, she'd swapped the thick plaid shirt for a sleeveless vest that showed off her strong arms and firm muscles to perfection.

"I'm sorry; I...I didn't mean to..." The words dried in my throat as Cassie dropped the handful of clothes and advanced toward me. I immediately broke eye contact and hung my head, falling easily into the familiar role of submissive, my body on fire in anticipation of the pain-pleasure combination to follow if Cassie's demeanor delivered on its promise.

"Look at me, Bryana." Cassie hooked one finger under my chin and forced my head up. I wrinkled my nose at the faint aroma of horses overlaid with sandalwood soap that lingered on her skin.

"Open your eyes." Gone was the soft lilt of earlier, replaced by an authoritative tone that commanded obedience and respect.

I obeyed. What else could I do? My brain was programmed to follow orders from a Domme.

Cassie's fingernail scored a path down my throat and into the valley between my breasts, drawing a gasp from my lips. A rush of arousal flooded my cunt with hot juices.

"You want to play?" Cassie held me hostage with her hypnotic gaze. I couldn't breathe properly.

I nodded, mutely. There was never a question in my mind.

"Say it… *Out loud.* Tell me what you want."

"I want to play," I confirmed, my voice barely above a whisper.

"Do you know what you're getting into?" There was a hint of irritation in her voice.

Do I?

Can I place my trust in a complete stranger?

I'd never thought twice about playing with a total stranger in a club, but this was a very different situation; here there would be no dungeon monitors on hand to protect me if the play got out of control. Common sense said I ought to call a halt now, while I still could. I opened my mouth to tell Cassie that I'd changed my mind. Then hysterical laugher bubbled up in my throat. Who was I kidding? This had gone way past the point of no return. Even though she had yet to do anything specific, Cassie had somehow turned me into a jabbering wreck begging for release from the torment raging within both mind and body.

"Yes…"

"Do you have a safe word?"

Oh God! A safe word… An ice-cold shower of reality doused the flames of desire in an instant.

Where is my common sense?

I stepped back, distancing myself from Cassie, practically gagging on the nausea rising in my throat. Furious that I'd let myself get carried away on a raft of sexual fantasies and ignored every single rule on safety, something I never, ever, did.

Nobody knew my whereabouts, there wasn't anybody to tell now and yet, I'd almost given a total stranger permission to tie me up and render me helpless, at the mercy of any pervert who might frequent this dungeon of dark desires.

"F...Fennel…My safe word is fennel."

"Fennel… Right." Cassie nodded. "Mine is piper. Now that we've got the essentials out of the way, are you game to carry on?"

"I...I'm…" I balked at giving my consent; although the fact that Cassie had checked for a safe word did allay some of my fears.

"In case you're wondering..." Cassie edged forward like a tiger on the prowl while her intense feline gaze betrayed her own hunger as she closed the gap between us. "It's just you and me, lover, so you're quite safe here – or as safe as you want to be."

"Yeah, right…" I waved my hand around the dungeon. "Do you honestly expect me to believe you have all this stuff set up for your own amusement or on the off chance that you might pick up a stranded motorist who's into both women and kink?" I wasn't totally stupid, or naïve. This quantity and quality of equipment pointed toward a professional setup and that meant more people. I didn't fancy being the victim of a gangbang or a porno film – not that I'd seen any sign of cameras but it stood to reason there were some around to catch the action.

"On the contrary." Cassie's laugh echoed off the walls. "All this is legit. I host regular house parties for the initiated and sometimes rent the entire castle out to very special clients who require total anonymity for their rich and famous guests. It helps pay for the upkeep and provides me with some fun as well."

"Really…" My gaze swept away from Cassie to skim the dungeon; my mouth dried as I pictured the fun and games that went on in here. So maybe she was telling the truth and it was just the two of us. Could I take the chance?

"Don't sound so surprised. From the look of excitement on your face when I found you exploring, I'd say you're pretty familiar with every bit of equipment on display."

"Yes, but…" In truth I was only really familiar a small number of the items. I'd seen a few more pieces in use at Out of Bounds, the BDSM club where Esmée hung out and to which she had introduced me, but only at a distance. My experience may be limited but my interest in the lifestyle wasn't.

"But nothing." Cassie sidled closer. Why don't you admit you can't wait to submit to me? It's written on your face…in your eyes."

Is it?

Could Cassie really see beyond my nagging doubt, to the smoldering desire for satisfaction? Weeks of neglect by Esmée had left me a frustrated wreck. Was the discovery of her betrayal reason enough to seek solace in the arms of another? Or entrust my safety to a complete stranger?

I scanned Cassie's face searching for reassurance, maybe something in her eyes that spoke of caring or trust. I found nothing, yet my hunger drove me forward.

As if drawn by an invisible elastic thread to the gorgeous butch in front of me, I closed the remaining distance until I felt Cassie's breath on my face. Our eyes met and locked in a heart-stopping moment of total oneness. Heat crawled up my neck and flooded my cheeks, and the air hissed out of my lungs cleansing me of all doubts and fears. I took one pace back, and then lowered my gaze in acknowledgement of my submissive role.

Cassie needed no further invitation. With a flick of her wrist, she stripped the towel from my body, tossed it aside, and then paced back and forth. I squirmed under the intense scrutiny, unused to standing totally naked before my Mistress, yet turned on by the sensual heat of her gaze. A new experience for me since Esmée had adopted a totally different approach to domination. Juices flooded my pussy and began to trickle down my thighs.

I held my breath when Cassie finally stopped pacing and approached the table. I watched, fascinated as she began to sort through the whips and floggers, taking her time, humming a quiet tune as if she was alone in her own world.

What instrument of delicious torture would she choose?

After what seemed an agonizingly long wait, Cassie finally selected the very same red spaghetti-string flogger that I had handled earlier. The satisfying zing-thwack which echoed around the dungeon when she tested it against wood turned my legs to jelly.

"I think we'll start there." Cassie waved the flogger in the direction of the stool. "Face down. No…Wait!"

Already halfway to my destination, I stopped with my heart in my mouth. I turned around slowly, waiting, expectant, anticipating the exhilarating lash of leather thongs against my bare skin.

"Put these on."

My slow reaction meant I barely managed to catch the set of nipple clamps and beaded mask that Cassie tossed in my direction. I took my time clipping the clover clamps onto my nipples, the heavy connecting chain hung almost to my waist and gave a satisfying tug as I moved. And once I'd pulled the mask over my face, I was relieved to discover I could still see, albeit through very thin slits that severely limited my field of vision. Being in total darkness was the one thing I feared above all else. Esmée had loved to test my devotion to the limit with sensory deprivation.

I stepped forward on unsteady legs, lowered myself into the restraints at the front of the stool, and then slid my body across the curved top with my arms stretched out above my head so that my wrists rested in the open manacles.

Other than my ragged breathing, not a sound broke the silence.

When Cassie clicked the thigh restraints shut locking me into the stool, I reveled in that special moment, the subtle rise in tension and a promise of the erotic pleasures to come if I could hold out long enough. As though she'd read my mind, Cassie adjusted the angle of the supports forcing my legs wider apart. Cool air caressed my moist heat like a lover's kiss and cranked my arousal up a further notch. In desperation, I pressed my mound hard against the stool and wriggled my ass.

"Stop that. You will wait until I give you permission to come." A sharp crack rent the air, and an exquisite pain seared my ass. I jerked in reaction, and the nipple clamps bit into my flesh, firecrackers exploding throughout my body. They'd barely ceased when Cassie snapped the wrist manacles shut completing my entrapment.

Oh, it felt so good.

Until this moment, I hadn't realized how much I'd missed the thrill and satisfaction I got from being shackled, flogged, and fucked senseless by a hard mistress. Esmée's supposedly heavy workload, or more likely her blossoming affair with that sly bitch, Marisa, had kept us away from the club for all of three months so I had a lot of time to make up for. My heartbeat raced out of control as the rush of blood pumped through my veins and hot juices scalded my throbbing crotch.

Cassie strutted around the stool; her soft leather boots making little sound on the oak floor. With each circuit, she teased the flogger across my skin: up my legs and down my back, across my ass so the strands licked at my slit like a tongue and got slicker with my juices at each sensuous stroke. I grew even hotter and wetter; my excitement and anticipation rose to a fever pitch until I hovered on the brink of the forbidden orgasm. And when Cassie thrust a hard dildo deep into my slick pussy, I came apart.

My eager muscles claimed the cold steel with a vice-like grip. I thrashed against the restraints and the stool as wave after wave of electric sensation drove me higher and further until I plunged over the precipice into a place I'd never been before – floating weightless in space, enveloped in bright rainbow lights with the crash of waves pounding a distant shore filling my ears. I fought to prolong the ecstasy, to stay forever in this perfect world, but the colors and sounds faded all too soon leaving me slumped over the stool, my breathing ragged, and my body twitching with aftershocks.

"I didn't give you permission to come, bitch!" Cassie said, voicing her displeasure. She did a couple of circuits around the stool, flicking the flogger against her boot, making me wait to discover my fate. "Now I shall have to punish you, and then we'll start over again, from the beginning."

Bring it on. I heard the whoosh a split second before the flogger connected with my ass. I screamed, bucking, as the dying pulses of my orgasm were rejuvenated, raising me to fresh heights of pleasure.

Oh God! This felt so good. I relaxed, allowing the waves of incredible sensation to flow through my body.

And this was just the start; Cassie's words held the promise of a fun-filled night.

Slave to Lust

Bryana

*Can Bryana risk letting Cassie Stuart
back into her life?*

"**A**t *last!*"

I didn't immediately recognize the gravelly voice that echoed like the crack of a whip through the silent lobby. For a few timeless seconds the sounds merely reverberated around my head, while my brain refused to process the information. Then my gaze focused on the figure seated on the floor right outside my door and reality disintegrated into fantasy.

Cassie Stuart's appearance in my world, both unexpected and unannounced, defied belief. She slowly uncurled her legs and got to her feet. Although much the same height, with me wearing heels, her aura of domination gave the impression that she towered over me.

The shock of her presence set my heart hammering so hard it felt as if a massive locomotive was tearing a path through my chest. From the little I knew of Cassie, she would want to exert herself, her authority, her dominant position and in return, she'd expect me to submit myself totally to her will.

Fuck! I didn't need her or that sort of intense pressure in my life right now.

I caught my breath and allowed the instinct for flight to gain the upper hand. If I could just distance myself from her and from temptation then I'd… The doors to the elevator chose that moment to swish shut behind me cutting off my escape route.

Even as a comparative novice in the world of Domme/sub, I knew it was a pipe dream to imagine that we could ever meet as equals. In the same context there were too many obstacles in the way of us becoming friends, or lovers, in the conventional sense. I still had a lot to learn about being submissive and, to be honest, I wasn't entirely convinced that Cassie was the right Mistress to guide me through to the next stage. Did I even want to try? Yes, no, maybe… I lambasted myself. Being indecisive was getting me nowhere.

She drilled me a penetrating gaze. "Where have you been, Bryana?"

The question sounded more like an accusation. I frowned, trying to get a handle on where Cassie was coming from since we hadn't seen each other or communicated in more than six months. Had she expected to find me sitting around, waiting, like an obedient puppy for her to get in touch?

"Paris. I…" The half answer tumbled from my lips in a strangled gasp. She had me so flustered and confused I couldn't breathe properly, let alone speak. I dropped my bags and my gaze.

How did she find me?

A very good question. In a final attempt to sever all ties with the past and my faithless ex, Esmée Vincent, I'd moved into this new apartment in a rapidly expanding Docklands complex just four weeks ago, although, recent events had proved that Esmée wasn't so easy to dismiss from my life. The grapevine in Paris had been abuzz with talk of her and that haughty, stick-insect, Marisa, the model with whom she'd shacked up even before our affair ended. According to the rumor mill, their fledgling relationship had already hit the rocks with both parties choosing to bad-mouth me all over the show as a way of absolving themselves from blame for their sorry debacle. Not that I'd had any part in their current predicament. Word had it that Esmée, apparently never satisfied with what she had and always seeking greener grass, was caught, in flagrante delicto, fucking the avant-garde designer, Angel Z, during an after-show party. Marisa's revenge came with the swift, decisive and very public seduction of Yazmin, Angel Z's current favorite companion. I sighed. Why was I even bothering to rake up the past or waste my time thinking about those stupid, self-serving, bitches? Esmée and Marisa deserved each other and I deserved...

Cassie?

I lifted my gaze; briefly scanning her weather-beaten face before moving down over her lean body. Whew! Even that brief appraisal left me needing a cold shower. Her jeans and the green plaid shirt worn over a toned pale green vest were a little neater than I recalled and, presumably as a concession to London, a pair of Cuban-heeled ankle boots had replaced the black and tan knee-length riding boots. Otherwise, she hadn't changed at all from the sexy butch who had ridden to my rescue after the Jaguar ran out of road and into a peat bog in the wilds of Scotland. Cassie was the hottest butch I'd come across in my entire life. There was no denying she had all the attributes to attract women in droves so she didn't need to chase a nonentity like me.

My body trembled in a cross between excitement and fear at the thought of being pursued by Cassie. I didn't want to get involved with her, or with anybody. What I needed was a break. Time alone to be myself. To regroup and find a new direction to take my life.

"Who were you fucking in Paris?"

Why did she assume I was out on the fuck?

Did I come across as a bitch in heat prepared to fuck anybody and everybody?

I sucked in a long calming breath to prevent myself from responding before I'd given my brain and mouth time to synchronize. Cassie had no jurisdiction over me, or my actions; other than those occasions when…if…we ever came together in a Domme/sub situation. Nor had she any right to invade my privacy. After consideration, I chose to ignore her intrusive question and ask a couple of my own instead.

"Why are you here?" I met her dark brooding gaze with uncharacteristic boldness. "What do you want from me?" The obvious response, one that would put my mind at rest, would be 'let's have a return session then we'll call it quits' or something along those lines.

"What do you think?" Cassie's brow rose with the question. "Did you honestly think I'd just let you walk away from me like that, without permission?" Her tone of voice, backed up by her body language, challenged me to argue the point. "Yeah, I know, you're wondering why it's taken me so long to find you?" She shrugged not waiting for me to respond before continuing. "You were a right bitch to track down; that's why."

Heat crawled across my skin. The memory of our one amazing night together resurfaced to ignite an inferno inside my guts. However, her assertion that she wasn't prepared to let me walk away from her overlooked the fact that I had done just that; and despite her claim to the contrary, Cassie probably hadn't tried very hard to find me. I shook my head. If she'd really wanted to track me down, she could have done so much sooner and without too much trouble since I hadn't exactly hidden myself away from the world. Why would I? The truth was much simpler. Following my pre-dawn flight from Auchtercairn, I had never expected to have any contact with Cassie again. Particularly as I hadn't even bothered to say goodbye or thank her for rescuing me from a cold wet night on the mountain.

I'd woken early, before five o'clock, the strange bed, and even stranger room, confusing my brain until the pleasant aches creeping across my body reminded me of the night's events. Not wanting to disturb anybody, particularly Cassie, I ventured downstairs in search of my bag and some clean underwear. Jazzy, my faithful Jaguar XJS convertible, stood in the courtyard where Hamish, Cassie's estate factor, had towed her in late the previous evening. Unbelievably, she looked pristine, freshly washed, and thankfully undamaged, with not a sign of her recent excursion into the peat bog remaining. *Nice man*; I silently thanked Hamish for the trouble he'd taken to clean her up. My hand glided lovingly across her silky smooth, metallic-silver bodywork then, from habit, I opened the door and slipped into the driver's seat. The familiarity of the padded leather seat cradled my frame and soothed my aches. Out of curiosity, I tried the starter and unbelievably the motor purred into life as if nothing untoward had happened. Without thinking of the consequences of my actions, I engaged drive then pulled cautiously out of the courtyard onto the narrow lane. Once underway, with both steering and brakes feeling normal, I drove on not stopping until I reached Inverness where I checked Jazzy into a workshop for a thorough inspection and myself into a spa hotel for a couple of nights of pampering before completing my journey South.

On my return to London, I'd set about the process of rearranging my life, looking to start afresh with no baggage and nothing to remind me of the past. However, the arrangements had taken a lot longer than I'd have liked mainly due to my punishing work schedule. These last few months had been particularly hectic, with photographic assignments all over the globe. It had also taken nearly four months to get shot of the expensive apartment in fashionable Chelsea that I'd leased to please Esmée then find and negotiate a satisfactory two year agreement on this new apartment. Two years would give me some breathing space and ample time to work out where my future lay. I wasn't even sure I wanted to make the UK my permanent home. Both Paris and Amsterdam, being on the European mainland where most of my photographic commissions were these days, had distinct advantages over London in terms of lifestyle and transportation links. So far, only one certainty was set in stone, no more sharing for me; the upheaval when a relationship failed was both emotionally and financially draining as well as time consuming. If I did become involved with somebody new then she would have to keep her own place.

Cassie hadn't been exactly forthcoming about her sudden reappearance in my life; I tried again. "I still don't understand why you've come."

"We have unfinished business."

"Have we?" I couldn't get my head around the fact that Cassie wanted more from me. Our one night together had been a fluke, a chance encounter, two strangers caught up in a wild sexual adventure then destined never to meet again. Cassie was way out of my league both socially and in terms of her sexual experience. That fully equipped dungeon in the tower at Auchtercairn was the stuff of fantasy. Few people could aspire to private ownership of such a wide selection of pleasure instruments. Besides which, I didn't want to get involved in a new relationship so soon after seeing the back of an old one, and inevitably the distance between us would prove an insurmountable obstacle to any permanent arrangement. Cassie's domain, her castle, Auchtercairn, was six hundred miles from London and a world away from my comfort zone.

The events of that night had tested me to the limit. Beginning with the way Cassie's hands glided up my thighs as she hiked my unsuitable pencil skirt up around my hips and helped me mount that disgusting, smelly, animal. I shuddered again, as I always do when I recall the sexual high I got while riding Tavish; the friction of the rough horse blanket against my crotch sent my libido spiraling out of control. Not to mention what followed. Hot! Cassie had proved herself worthy of the title Dominatrix; a true Mistress of Seduction. Looking back, I still can't believe how quickly I submitted to her will or that I had given so little thought to my own safety. It was a crazy chance to take with a total stranger. Neither could I fathom what she'd got out of the one-sided arrangement. Cassie had strapped my naked body to a bench and flogged several amazing orgasms out of me yet all the while, she had remained aloof, fully clothed, and never once allowed me to touch her.

"Yes, we do, and I've come to collect." Cassie flexed her shoulders, her mouth tightening into a fine line. "Why are we having this conversation out here? Aren't you going to invite me inside? I've spent most of the three last days sitting on this damned hard floor waiting for you to get home. I need a shower, a stiff drink, some food, and a good fuck, but not necessarily in that order."

"I'm sorry." Anxious not to incur Cassie's wrath, I leapt forward and swiped my keycard to release the door. Then I stood aside to allow her to enter first.

I couldn't begin to imagine what she would make of the apartment, or the austere modernity, after the faded elegance of Auchtercairn. In choosing the theme for my new start in life, I'd settled for minimalistic simplicity in both the décor and furnishings, with the starkness of black and white relieved by very few dashes of vibrant color in the shape of artwork and silk flowers. I slipped out of my shoes and followed in Cassie's wake as she strode across the living area; the tap-tap of her heels sounded ominous, like the measured drumbeat of an executioner, upon the hardwood floor. She stopped at the picture window, taking time to absorb the view of the Thames with the O2 arena opposite and the hazy outline of the Thames Barrier away in the distance. Then she turned to assess the room with a long sweeping glance before she nodded.

"Nice."

She liked it!

That one word of approval meant everything to me. I expelled a pent up breath and waited for more; there was bound to be more. What would Cassie do or say next?

"Come here."

Nervous tension tied my stomach into tight knots but I obeyed her softly spoken command, moving toward her without question, my gaze trained on the floor. I stopped inches from her, close enough to feel her breath on my face, and waited for her next move.

Cassie reached out, swept me into her arms and sealed my lips in a kiss. That drugging kiss did for me, and for any lingering hope of severing my involvement with her. I could no longer kid myself that I had the strength of will to resist temptation or keep my distance from Cassie. Then she swung me around and thrust me hard up against the window, I felt a vibration ripple through the glass as she trapped me in place with her solid body. Her hot lips left my mouth, traveled slowly down to suck and bite at the soft flesh of my throat. I became dizzy, losing complete track of time and space, as if I was being whirled on a carousel. Heat coursed through my veins and gravitated to my crotch. Then her hand found the hem of my skirt and her fingers glided slowly up my stockinged thigh until they encountered bare flesh. The significance of her action, harking back to the day we met, didn't escape me; it merely increased the tension. Violent trembles shook my body. Unbelievably, I was on the point of orgasm by the time she stroked her fingers across my silk panties and then cupped my mound in the palm of her hand. Cassie cut off my strangled gasp with her lips then she drove her tongue into my mouth and pressed the heel of her hand hard against my clit in a simultaneous assault that tipped me over the edge in seconds.

The orgasm seemed endless. My legs turned to jelly, losing all their strength. I was glad of Cassie's support, without which I was in danger of collapsing into a heap onto the floor. I couldn't get my head around this amazing orgasm or the speed with which it had overtaken me. For some unfathomable reason, Cassie had the ability to turn me on like no other woman I'd known. None of the women I'd been with in the past six months, since Esmée's departure from my life, had had anything like this effect on my libido. In fact, I hadn't even come close to an orgasm during the last couple of private sessions with Sasha at Out of Bounds. That in itself was definitely odd. I'd known Sasha a long time, we were perfectly attuned to one another and usually had really hot sex together but not lately. Something was missing; the will was there but the spark of desire failed to ignite into a flame. Maybe the break-up with Esmée had affected me more than I thought but then along came Cassie and wham! She hardly had to touch me before fireworks exploded along with a powerful orgasm.

Cassie broke contact with my mouth and withdrew her hand from the now damp silk covering my sex. Then she took a step back from me. A flash of even white teeth signaled a triumphant grin.

She knew!

Somehow, Cassie had read my mind, she had gained access to my most secret thoughts, and was taking pleasure from that knowledge that she, alone, had the power to draw something extraordinary from me and propel me into orbit in the process.

"Now I need a stiff drink." Cassie scanned the room, a slight frown creasing her brow.

If she was looking for evidence of a bar, or a drinks cabinet, she'd be sorely disappointed.

"Do you have any single malt?"

I shook my head. "I don't keep any spirits, just wine." At least, I hoped I had a bottle of wine tucked away in the kitchen cupboard. I hardly ever drank alcohol at home, and never alone.

"Wine will have to do, for now." Cassie sighed. "We can stock up at the liquor store later."

It was my turn to frown. That last remark sounded as if Cassie planned to hang around for a while. How long? By her own admission, she'd already been in London at least three days and maybe longer. Didn't she have an estate to run, dogs and horses to exercise, etc?

"You are planning to stay…in London?" I almost said here, but I didn't want to presume, or give her ideas, and besides, it was a reasonable assumption as she didn't have any bags with her, that she must have used a hotel or an apartment for the past few nights.

"I had hoped that you'd offer me a bed." Cassie gave me a long intense stare that twisted my stomach into knots. "I'm sort of homeless for the next few weeks."

"Why? How come? What about—"

"I have a film crew in the castle. They're shooting an erotic horror movie. Definitely not my scene. I can't stomach all the fake blood and gore these films use." Cassie shuddered theatrically, her grimace alone speaking volumes. "Nor do I relish the prospect of meeting a horny stud on the staircase late at night. Hamish will look after the horses and the dogs, and Effie, his wife, will take care of everything else. Meanwhile, I get to play with you."

She might have asked first.

I didn't fancy being treated like a toy, to be picked up and discarded at will. After all, we were still virtual strangers; our only link a few hours of sexual pleasure. Although the prospect of expanding on that experience was undeniably tempting and I didn't object in principle to us getting it on together, I wasn't sure I wanted to share my space with her twenty-four-seven.

For once, I stood my ground. "How long are we talking about?" This was real life, not a Domme/sub scene where I was bound to obey my Mistress without question. "I have less than two weeks at home before I'm due to go away again."

Cassie huffed loudly, her displeasure at my boldness evident in the dark glare she bestowed upon me. "The film crew has an eight week lease starting last Monday, with a two week optional extension which I hope they take up as I'm counting on the extra money to complete a major roof repair."

Really!

Another seven weeks minimum and maybe more. I didn't want to appear uncharitable, especially after she'd taken me in when I needed a bed but being put in a position where I could hardly refuse to repay the favor tenfold irked. It felt as if she was taking advantage of me. However, I needed to make some sort of decision, and fast.

"Very well, you can stay for the time being…for the next ten days…until I leave for Amsterdam. We can have a rethink then."

"Thank you." Cassie favored me with another grin. "That's the accommodation settled; now what about the wine you promised me?"

"Sorry… I'll get it now."

Why did Cassie always manage to make me feel guilty?

I hurried across to the open-plan kitchen area and dug into a cupboard finally coming up with a bottle of Châteauneuf-du-Pape for my pains. Thankfully, it was a good quality wine and, being a robust fruity red, didn't need chilling. I poured a couple of glasses and handed the generous measure to Cassie keeping the smaller one for myself then I racked my brains about what I could offer her for dinner. My freezer wasn't as well stocked as I'd have liked – I hadn't had time to do any serious shopping since moving in. However, there were several restaurants within walking distance that catered for all cuisines, preferences, and prices, so we wouldn't starve. When consulted, Cassie expressed a preference for a traditional steak with all the trimmings, which made the choice of eatery simple. I hardly ever eat red meat but Cardon's, the local steakhouse, also did a wonderful fish platter so we'd both be satisfied. With our dining option settled, I phoned ahead to book a table since I knew they were always busy and I hated queuing.

After finishing her glass of wine and a top-up, Cassie left to retrieve her bags from wherever she'd left them and presumably settle her account. Which gave me a chance to change into a casual outfit, T-shirt and leggings, unpack my bags, start the laundry and generally get organized for having company. Then I slipped downstairs to do a bit of essential breakfast shopping at the local convenience store. She was back within the hour carrying a surprisingly small bag considering the length of time she planned to be away from home. Her needs were obviously simple compared to mine; limited clothes, no cosmetics and none of the bulky photographic equipment which I was forced to lug around everywhere I went.

I spent a few minutes giving Cassie a tour of the apartment, finishing up at the second bedroom, her room, which prompted a raised eyebrow. However, I drew the line at sharing my personal space with a virtual stranger even if I did want her to fuck me senseless. I left Cassie to settle in and when I returned a few minutes later with some spare towels, it was something of a surprise to find a trail of discarded garments that led me to the en suite bathroom where she was already in shower.

Oh my God! My body fizzed into instant awareness. She had her back to me. I stood in the bathroom doorway feasting my eyes on the sight of water cascading over her tight ass. Since I hadn't seen her naked during our previous encounter, the firm, well-toned, muscles were something of a pleasant surprise. My fingers itched for a camera to record this hot butch at her ablutions. The towels slipped from my grasp and I pressed my hand to my crotch savoring the throbbing heat. I don't know if I cried out or made a sudden movement but something attracted her attention and before I knew what had happened she'd opened the screen and dragged me, fully dressed, into the shower with her. The force of the spray on my clothed body felt distinctly odd yet exhilarating and very erotic. It appeared that, with Cassie around, it didn't take much to turn me on, after all.

"Here." She handed me a bar of fragrant sandalwood soap. "Wash me." I began to lather her skin moving easily over most of her body while avoiding certain areas for fear of going too far and incurring her wrath. Then Cassie grabbed hold of a handful of my hair, pushing down until I got the message and knelt in front of her, my face level with her crotch.

Much as I wanted to part Cassie's labia and explore her intimate area, I hesitated to begin until she gave me permission to proceed. Eventually Cassie put me out of my misery by reaching for my hand and guiding it to her sex. She was so big, so hard. I stroked her clit, my touch hesitant and clumsy as if I was a complete novice getting my first taste of sex play. Cassie murmured approval. Emboldened by her encouragement, I slid two fingers into her cunt and pushed deep, my thumb making contact with her clit with each inward thrust.

Cassie groaned then twisted my hair bringing my face closer to her sex. "You want to lick me off?"

"Yes." In my heightened state of lust, I didn't need a second invitation.

"Yes what?"

Her angry growl brought me up short. In my eagerness to obey her and get started, I was forgetting my manners.

"Yes, Mistress."

"That's better." She widened her stance and thrust her pelvis toward me. "Suck it, bitch."

I buried my face in her crotch, sucked her clit into my mouth and circled the rock hard flesh teasing the tip with my tongue while I continued thrusting my fingers into her wet hole.

Cassie's legs started to tremble, the vibrations increasing as her orgasm approached. She reached down and tore my hand from her cunt. "Use your tongue; fuck me hard, make me come. Now!"

Happy to oblige, I abandoned her clit, licking my way across the soft flesh to her slit. I held her thighs apart and drove into her moist heat. Over and over, I thrust deep and hard, curling my tongue to sweep the walls of her cunt as I withdrew.

"Yes!" She moved with me, her breath rasped. Faster and faster, we became as one, driving toward release, searching for the ultimate pinnacle of total satisfaction. Cassie came first. A flood of hot, honeyed, liquid hit my tongue milliseconds before my own release exploded in an awesome, muscle-clenching, burst of sweet agony. I lapped at her pussy juice, eager not to miss a drop.

"That's enough. Get up, you dirty little bitch."

A swishing sound cut through the air and something slapped me across the back hard enough to sting even through my wet T-shirt. I scrambled to my feet, backed away from Cassie until I came up against the tiled wall of the shower stall. Pulses of my fading orgasm continued to ripple through my body.

"Did you think you could take advantage of my good nature?" She fired the question like a bullet straight at my head.

How did I take advantage?

I tried to regulate my breathing downward and get my brain working again.

"I'll overlook your presumption, just this once." Cassie shut off the spray and smoothed her hands over her short dark hair to squeegee the excess water away from her face. "However, in future, I won't tolerate your insatiable greed. Self control and abstinence are both part of your life from now on, you must practice them at all times. You will only come when I say you can. Is that understood?"

"Yes, Mistress. I will obey your command." I hung my head in submission and tried to envisage how her caveat would affect me. How could I not have an orgasm when my body demanded release? Was it even possible to resist the natural progress of sexual desire, to halt the race for gratification and completion?

"Make sure you do." Cassie swung the screen open, and stepped out of the shower stall. She grabbed a large towel off the heated rail and draped it across her shoulders then she nodded to the pile of fallen towels. "And get this mess cleared up!"

I bent down to pick them up and she slapped me across the ass. "Now, go and dress yourself, I want my dinner."

Carrying the bundle of towels, I padded across the hallway to my room where I stripped and took the briefest of showers to freshen up, and then wrapped a towel around my body, sarong fashion, while I dried my hair. Cardon's wasn't a dressy place, smart casual was accepted as the norm but I liked to keep up certain standards. Thankful that I was an expert at the quick change, I selected fresh silk underwear and a simple black two-piece from Giovanni d'Marco's prêt-à-porter range. Hair, makeup and perfume completed, I was done in a little over fifteen minutes from start to finish.

"You're ready!" Cassie actually sounded impressed when she found me waiting for her in the living room. She still wore jeans and those Cuban heels, although she'd replaced the green shirt of earlier with a dark plum-red one worn over a black vest. The darker colors flattered her skin tone and enhanced her butch sexiness. I'd have to persuade her into letting me do a photo session, both clothed and unclothed. Thoughts of doing the naked bits, especially a shower scene, sent my pulse racing wildly but mindful of her rules I fought to control myself. Cassie did things to my libido that defied reasoning. With her in my life, I was little more than a slave to lust.

"Shall we go?" I picked up my purse and slipped my feet into the matching shoes I'd left ready by the door. "The restaurant is only a short walk."

"Wait!" Cassie suddenly stopped in her tracks around half distance between the apartment and Cardon's. I glanced around to see her disappearing into the liquor store. I turned and followed her into the store where I found her deep in discussion with the assistant over the merits of different single malts.

A while later, once we were seated in the steak house with our order taken, I queried her eventual choice of the three tissue wrapped bottles that she'd carried in a bag to our destination. Not being much of a drinker myself, I thought it excessive. "Do you drink a lot of whisky?"

Cassie laughed at my ignorance. "No, to put your mind at rest I'm not an alcoholic, I'm a connoisseur. Single malt is a fascinating spirit, all malts use the same basic ingredients but the end result is subtly different from one distillery to the next. There are hundreds of distilleries and therefore a wealth of different tastes to savor and enjoy. Rather like wines in a way, where you get subtle nuances between wines made from the same grape variety but in different years or vineyards." She topped up my glass from the bottle of Merlot she'd ordered to go with our food. "I must educate your palate."

"You can try." I wasn't sure I had a palate for spirits but maybe Cassie could teach me as part of my general education.

Fuck! What was I thinking? Turning this transient arrangement into some sort of permanent relationship. I must be mad, or bad... Yes, definitely bad where Cassie was concerned.

Over dessert of a rich chocolate gateau served with both cream and ice cream – it turned out Cassie had a very sweet tooth – she raised the question of my experience or lack thereof. "Judging by your response to my playroom, I gather you've attended a club or a party where that sort of equipment has been available but I'm not sure you've actually used any of it. Would that be a fair assessment?"

I nodded. "Yes, I belong to a private club – Out of Bounds – I've been a member for a few years now and although I keep up my membership I don't go there very often. I'm not...I haven't been very adventurous with the equipment. Also, just for the record, I know nothing about being in a proper Domme/sub relationship which is where I think we're headed."

Cassie gave me a rare smile. "I appreciate your honesty, honey." Another spoonful of the rich confection disappeared into her mouth. "Mmmm, I've heard of that place; it has a good name. Would you propose me as a member? I need a proper workout to calm me down so I don't frighten the shit out of you when we get physical."

It was my turn to smile. "Of course I'll propose you. I can also sign you in as my guest while you're waiting for your membership to come through."

"Thanks." Cassie pushed her empty plate aside and eyed my half eaten blueberry cheesecake. "Are you going to finish that?"

I shook my head. "No, desserts aren't really my thing." I'd only ordered it to keep her company. Before I could blink, Cassie had whipped my plate across to her side and cleared the contents. How did she keep so trim, so fit, with her love of sweet things? Sex? No, probably all her outdoor activities, exercising the horses and dogs.

It was still early, barely eight thirty, I watched Cassie stir sugar into her second cup of coffee and drink the sickly-sweet brew. The rest of the evening needed some thought and as this was my home turf, I decided it was up to me to suggest something in the way of entertainment. Out of Bounds stayed open until two AM. on week nights, plenty of time to give her a guided tour and get her membership organized.

"Would you care to take a look at the club tonight?"

"Nah, I'm fucked." Cassie signaled for our server to bring the bill then she leaned across the table. "Talking of fucking…how about we go back to the apartment and work off some of this food in bed? Meanwhile, I will put some thought into your training. We should get to know each other a whole lot better before we go anywhere near the club and the serious stuff."

"Yes, please." I liked her idea, a lot. Thoughts of what we might do in bed together ratcheted up the tension. As well as satisfying my increasing sexual need, it made sense to find our level of understanding so I'd feel comfortable putting my trust in her no matter what she did or how she constrained me.

"Good." Cassie nodded. "I'm sure you'll be a diligent pupil." She paid the bill with her gold card and we swapped the well lit restaurant for the somewhat darker streets. I enjoyed the feeling of togetherness when she took my arm to steer me through the crowds, as we hurried back to the apartment both eager for what was to come. I sincerely hope there wasn't a CCTV camera in the elevator to witness to our outrageous behavior. We were so busy touching and kissing that we almost missed our arrival at the seventh level. Once inside the apartment, Cassie dragged me straight into her room. Our frantic kisses hiked the temperature up another good few notches. Then, suddenly, she withdrew and held me away from her.

"Undress me!"

Her sharp command and stern expression jolted me back to reality. After a pleasant evening out, we were suddenly back to Domme/sub rules.

"Yes, Mistress." I sprang into action, starting with the buttons on her shirt. Once I'd dragged the sleeves off her arms, I lifted the vest up and over her head. She wasn't wearing a bra, her tits were small and firm and didn't need support. I kissed and licked my way down her body then dropped to my knees in front of her. My fingers were clumsy as I fumbled with the button and zipper on her jeans but I eventually won and pushed the denim down her legs then helped her to step out of both jeans and boots.

Lordy, lordy! I regarded her final garment. The black briefs were so...

Hot!

I moistened my lips, hooked my thumbs into the elastic and eased the underwear down her thighs. With my face close to her crotch, I could smell her need, the musky aroma turned me on big time. Saliva flooded my mouth and I leaned forward to…

"Get up, bitch!"

Mortified, I did as instructed, bitterly disappointed that she hadn't given me a chance to taste her. Instead, she left me standing, isolated in the middle of the room while she strolled nonchalantly away and settled herself into a comfortable reclining position on the bed.

"Strip for me!" Her heated gaze raked my body turning my insides to liquid fire. "I want to see a proper striptease, the full works; show me what you can do."

Hell! Do I have the bottle to perform in front of her?

I didn't have any choice…I must do it or say goodbye to Cassie and whatever the future held for us. Besides which, Cassie would expect much more than that from me over the coming days and weeks as my training progressed. If I failed this simple test, our relationship would be history and, even on such short acquaintance, I couldn't bear for that to happen.

Night Games

Cassie

Danger lurks in the dark recesses of Out Of Bounds. Will Cassie be able to save Bryana from harm?

"**S**trip for me!"

I reclined on the bed, naked, contemplating Bryana standing before me, whilst I hastily revised my view of her experience and therefore the direction that this evening might take from here.

Bryana's reaction had completely thrown me. Indecision writ large on her face, she shifted her feet uneasily, as if poised for instant flight. How could anybody change so much in so short a time? She was a totally different person now from the hot, sexy, woman who'd practically let me fuck her in a public elevator less than an hour ago. Or, for that matter, the one who'd climaxed so readily with just the pressure of my hand against her silk covered sex earlier today. Now she appeared awkward, hesitant, or even downright reluctant to do as I asked.

Although Bryana had been perfectly frank concerning her level of experience specifically regarding the BDSM lifestyle, based on our previous encounter, I'd expected her to show a modicum of understanding when asked to do something. To be honest, though, I hadn't really taken her claim to know anything about D/s relationships at face value. She wasn't stupid; I was certain she knew the basic rules of the game. More likely, she was simply being modest or covering herself in advance for any slips. Anyway, I scoffed, this wasn't rocket science; she didn't need any knowledge of D/s protocol to perform a sexy strip for her lover; something like that should come as second nature.

My gaze raked Bryana from head to toe. God, she was a beautiful creature. So elegant, too. That understated black two-piece clothed her gorgeous body so perfectly it might have been designed especially for her – well, when one considered her career and the top designers with whom she associated, in all probability it had been. Black suited her; it enhanced the creamy perfection of her skin, and brought out the golden highlights in her hair. I couldn't get enough of her but that didn't mean I was prepared to go soft and allow her to call the tune. If we were to have a future together, she had to learn obedience, and how to behave. The first step on our road to understanding must be trust. Bryana needed to understand where I was coming from and that even though I might push the boundaries of our relationship from time to time I would never ask her for anything more than she was willing to give.

Bryana shook her head, seemingly lost for words.

Now we'd come so far, I wasn't prepared to back down, it wouldn't serve any purpose except to confuse the issue. She must show a little good faith, place her trust in me and pass this first simple test before we could move forward onto the more serious stuff.

"I want to see a proper striptease, the full works; show me what you can do." My mouth dried, and anticipation set my heart pounding as I silently willed her to obey me.

Yet with Bryana's apparent awkwardness and uncertainty, one could almost be forgiven for thinking that this was her first time and she had no idea how to strip for the pleasure of displaying her body.

Could it be?

No, I mentally shrugged, she wasn't a virgin in the recognized sense of the word. My research into her background had returned a string of past lovers. However, it didn't follow that any of those bitches were fully paid up Dommes. I also knew, for a fact, that she liked being whipped to an orgasm: the sexy little wench had proven that point by coming apart before my eyes when I introduced a light spaghetti-string flogger and a dildo into our only dungeon workout. At the time, I felt sure she'd have been up for much more, maybe even a session on the cross, but she ran out on me before I could test my theory. I'd still not discovered why she fled from Auchtercairn in the middle of the night like she did. There'd been no clue in her behavior before we went to bed. In fact I'd got the impression that she'd be happy to stay the whole weekend.

Just when I'd almost given up in despair, she finally raised her hands to undo the topmost button on her jacket. One by one, she slipped the tiny iridescent spheres through almost invisible buttonholes until the two halves of the garment parted. She dropped her hands to her sides giving me sight of a bare midriff and a black lace bra that cupped her to perfection, lifting the soft creamy flesh into a tantalizing cleavage. I focused on the rise and fall of her breasts, accentuated by her rapid breathing, and moistened my lips, almost tasting her on my tongue in the process. I had plans for those exquisite breasts but first I needed to get her naked, and totally tuned to one path, serving my needs.

"Come on, Bryana, stop messing about. You're testing my patience." I waved my hand to demonstrate what I wanted. "Lose that top, now!"

"Cassie, I…" She behaved as if she was scared of the consequences. The demons chasing each other across her lovely face were now glaringly obvious. Had somebody mistreated her in the past or had I made a monumental error and this was a simple case of inexperience?

Hell! Have I found myself a virgin, in the metaphorical sense?

The question backed me up, adding to my sense of disbelief. As a Dominatrix, I'd met all levels of experience bar one, the complete novice. Visitors to Auchtercairn, both my own guests and the varied groups who came to use my fully equipped dungeon, were already committed to the lifestyle and to whatever particular line of BDSM they followed. I sometimes joined them, or not, as the fancy took me. More often not these days, my appetite for the pleasures of the dungeon had become somewhat jaded by the same old routines with the same old submissive partners.

I had never before started from scratch with a clean sheet, a virgin canvas with which to work. If Bryana was that person, my life would be complete. My heart beat a little faster at the prospect of training her to follow my word, teaching her to be the perfect sub, my dream woman. That, of course, would take time and patience. Long discussions and ever harder tests of her devotion and her willingness to serve. For now, and for the immediate future, all I could envisage was taking small steps toward the greater goal.

Since we weren't making any progress with her first step, I tried a different, softer approach in a last ditch attempt to get things moving. "Bryana, honey, I know how much you want to remove your jacket." My voice crackled with the increased tension. "You want to do it to please me and, I can assure you, pleasing me will make you feel so good."

Bryana flashed me a startled glance before she lowered her gaze once more. With scarcely any movement, she shrugged the garment from her shoulders then allowed the soft fabric to glide slowly down her arms and drop to the floor.

"Now your skirt." I kept my voice even, without a hint of the irritation I felt at her obstinate refusal to yield more than an inch at a time.

Again, there was a slight hesitation before Bryana complied. She slid the zipper down and the skirt followed, the material whispering over silk clad legs to pool around her ankles. Black panties hugged her slim hips, the lacy fabric matching both her bra and the stocking tops.

Jeez! Moist heat pooled in my crotch and my nipples peaked. Bryana was trying my forbearance. I was sorely tempted to leap off the bed, grab her, and strip those sexy undergarments from her body then fuck her until she begged for mercy but that wouldn't move us forward. Patience had to be my watchword. I ran my hands lightly across my tits seeking some relief from the overwhelming ache of denial. I would get my reward soon enough.

I took a deep breath in an attempt to settle my nerves. "Turn around, slowly. Let me look at you."

She did as I commanded although I sensed a slight reluctance, or perhaps shyness, about her actions. No, I couldn't believe she suffered from shyness. I tried to recall how she'd behaved on our first, our only, night together but my memory of that event was a bit of a blur. I only remember she wore nothing but a towel when I came upon her exploring my dungeon and, in my eagerness to seize command of the situation, the towel soon disappeared. Who would have guessed all was not as it appeared? I could have sworn then that Bryana was fully aware of her place, both understanding and accepting the rules of the dungeon. Whatever her hang-up was, she would need to overcome it before we could move to the proper first stage of her training. I let her stand and reflect for a few minutes before I issued the next command.

"Remove your bra."

Bryana flinched, almost imperceptibly, and a soft gasp escaped her lips. After another significant pause, she reached around behind herself to unclip the fastening then slipped the straps down and off her arms. She dropped the flimsy scrap of lace onto the floor then straightened. Her ample breasts bounced seductively as she moved her hands to her sides close to the elastic of her panties. I noted with satisfaction that her nipples were already erect and begging me to attach the clamps that I had in a bag under the pillow but under the circumstances, those clamps had to wait awhile. Although we'd used a set during our night together at Auchtercairn, I didn't honestly think Bryana was ready for us to use them again, yet. First, I wanted to do something else. Something important, that would define our relationship and maybe help Bryana to see where I was coming from.

"Come here." I reached under the pillow, feeling around until my hand closed upon a long narrow box. I'd designed this item and had it handcrafted especially for Bryana. Now I hoped she would see my offering for what it was; an attempt on my part to reach an understanding, to signify a starting point and the first step on a long journey toward total commitment.

Bryana frowned, seemingly surprised that I hadn't asked her to remove her panties. She stepped out of the mess of clothes surrounding her feet and approached the bed.

"I have something for you." I raised the lid of the box. Bryana moved closer to look at the contents and a frown creased her brow as she ran a finger over the item inside. She took a deep breath, lifted the decorative choker from the box and examined the malleable silver braid that looked like an item of jewelry and would sit comfortably around her neck. Then she turned her attention to the Celtic symbol engraved on the silver clip that formed a centerpiece at the front. I'd based my design in part on one of the four emblems that appeared on my family crest. A three-point knot inside a circle to represent peace, understanding and unity. I hoped this ancient talisman would influence her emotional strength and help her achieve a perfect balance in thought, word and deed.

"It's beautiful…but…" Bryana fingered the fancy clip, opening and closing it several times, her expression troubled. "Umm…Is this what I think it is?"

I responded with my own question. "What do you think it is?" Since the sight of the collar clearly troubled her, I wanted to get to the root of the problem and felt it important to ask her to spell out what she thought it was, rather than having it come from me.

"A collar…for a sub…?" She gnawed at her lip.

I got the distinct impression that her first inclination was to throw the collar away, as far away as possible, but curiosity got the better of her.

"In principle, yes." I nodded and took a long breath in an attempt to slow my rapid heartbeat. "Do you understand what wearing it will represent?"

Bryana shot me a puzzled glance as if I was asking her to state the obvious. "That you own me… Once you fasten this around my neck, I am your slave."

"Not exactly." I smiled at her misconception. She clearly had a lot to learn, or more likely unlearn, about the D/s scene. "This is merely a Collar of Consideration, a first step to understanding where we are headed. As well as offering you some protection, it represents a serious intent on both our parts to explore this relationship and to see if it has a future but without the need to make any formal commitment. Think of it rather like a friendship ring. Either one of us may remove this collar at any time with no hard feelings or, in due course if everything goes well, we might move on to the next stage. The Training Collar carries more responsibility and a stronger bond. If you use the same analogy as before and think in terms of an engagement ring then you'll have some idea of the progression."

"Oh…I didn't know about the different levels." Bryana sounded awed. "I thought…" The shudder that accompanied her statement convinced me that somebody had made a very clumsy attempt at domination without taking care of her or the essential details along the way. This was obviously a serious hurdle to overcome. I silently cursed those idiots who crashed into the scene and took what they wanted without any thought for the victims or the broken lives they left behind. We would need to work through her fears and eliminate all the negative influences before progressing further.

"Bryana, honey." Having got her attention, I met and held her gaze then put her on the spot. "Will you wear this special collar for me?"

A look of horror momentarily clouded her gorgeous sapphire blue eyes.

"This is an important step forward for both of us," I tried to reassure her. "I want you to know that I will never intentionally do anything to hurt you or to cause you any harm, that's not what I'm about."

Bryana nodded. "Yes." Her hand shook as she handed me the collar. "Will you put it on for me, please?" She knelt down beside the bed and bundled her hair out of the way.

I fastened the collar around her neck, rejoicing in this breakthrough. Her acceptance of me as her protector, her tutor, and her lover warmed me. I hoped that in time she would want to play a permanent role in my life. This deserved a reward. I pulled her onto the bed and sealed our bargain with a kiss.

One kiss led to another, then another. The caress of her naked skin against mine raised the temperature several degrees and drove me wild with desire. I rolled her over and settled my body into her soft curves, my knee between her thighs, and deepened the kiss. Bryana sighed and opened her mouth to accept my tongue. She tasted wonderful, sweet and fruity, a combination of vanilla and wine. My hand sought her breast, and the nipple responded, swelling and hardening when I rolled it between my fingers. I moved to savor the nipple with my mouth, sucking hard then teasing the tip with my tongue.

"Yes, oh, yes." Bryana rocked her body against mine, spreading her legs, seeking better contact.

I slid one hand down to caress her thigh, sweeping the soft flesh, widening the circle until my fingers brushed lightly across her silk covered mound. Bryana jumped, her body coming off the bed then sinking back, as if I'd touched her with an electric cattle prod. My teeth grazed her nipple as I withdrew then I kissed and licked my way down her fragrant body, taking her panties down as I went, craving to bury myself in the moist heat of her femininity.

She met me full on, raising her pelvis, thrusting her clit into my mouth. In the throes of passion she was a different woman again; a hot, sexy wench who needed to be fucked long and hard. I pushed one finger into her slick heat then added a second and finally a third; her muscles encased my hand like a silken glove. She moaned softly, eagerly meeting and matching my thrusts. I nursed her clit, savoring her sweetness in my mouth and drove harder, pushing her toward a climax.

"Yes...Cassie!" Bryana screamed my name as she dissolved into a shuddering orgasm that seemed to go on forever. Then, thoroughly sated, she slept in my arms for the remainder of the night.

We arrived at Out of Bounds just after eight thirty. The taxi dropped us off outside a sprawling Victorian mansion situated on the edge of Hampstead Heath. Bryana signed me in as her guest then proceeded to give me a guided tour of the facilities. Having explored the main floor of the club that housed both a lounge bar and a dance floor, mostly unoccupied at this early hour, she led the way downstairs to the basement. The few people milling around were mostly staff; hosts, or dungeon monitors, who were available to answer questions, ensure safety, or demonstrate equipment to the members and guests. I didn't need any such help since most of the stuff available was familiar to me. However, Bryana stopped briefly to chat with the few people she knew and explain I was checking out the club prior to joining.

"Oh!" Bryana suddenly left my side and darted away to exchange air kisses with a statuesque brunette attired in a revealing black latex outfit and thigh-length boots, who occupied a small dimly lit alcove furnished with a couch and an impressive array of whips.

I shook my head at her impulsivity and followed in her wake then smiled when I got close enough to recognize an occasional visitor to Auchtercairn. She usually flew in to the castle for a long weekend bash with a group of high profile celebrity guests who always imported their own people to both staff the dungeon and to provide the entertainment.

"Cassie!"

"Sasha!"

We exclaimed in unison. I stepped forward to take the outstretched hand and exchange kisses with Sasha.

"Wow!" Bryana whooped in amazement. "You two already know each other." She turned to me, her eyes unusually luminous. "Sasha is not only a good friend, she's the wonderful person who gives me relief and restores my sanity."

"What a surprise." Sasha pumped my hand, then let her puzzled gaze drift from me to Bryana and back again. "I wouldn't have pictured you two as friends or... Not in a million years."

Or lovers, or...

I picked up Sasha's difficulty in defining our relationship. I imagine this would be the reaction of most people who knew me in the Scene, since the memory of Deanne, my last long-term submissive partnership was lost in the mist of time and I never paraded any of my real life friendships. The fact that Sasha also knew Bryana probably compounded her confusion.

Over the past few days, through our open and frank conversations, I'd established that Bryana was, as I'd already surmised, a complete novice. By all accounts, she had suffered greatly at the hands of a cruel manipulative, bitch who had fancied herself as a Domme but who had no proper knowledge or understanding of the D/s scene.

"We've know each other a while." I deliberately kept my response vague then waved one hand to encompass Sasha's domain. "And I wouldn't have expected to find you here."

"Touché." Sasha laughed. "It pays the bills. As Bryana will no doubt tell you, I'm a fixture in this little niche now and–" She stopped speaking abruptly and looked around frowning. "Where is Bryana? She was there a moment ago, then she just disappeared."

I spun around, my gaze sweeping over the large dungeon. Both the central space and the perimeter walls were dotted with equipment yet almost empty of people, as were most of the smaller specialist alcoves. I turned back to meet Sasha's concerned expression. "She can't have just disappeared. Maybe she went to the restroom." There had to be a logical explanation.

She nodded. "I sure hope so."

Sasha's uncertainty and her oddly worded remark had me worried. "What do you mean by that?"

"Nothing…it's just that Bryana has been having trouble with her ex…" Sasha bit her lip. "Ummm, I don't want to break any confidences. How much do you know about Bryana and her life?"

"Enough to know that she's been frightened out of her wits by some stupid bitch masquerading as a Domme."

Sasha shrugged. "That's the way of the world. It happens everywhere, even here, despite the checks we carry out on prospective club members. However, this is serious, the woman is evil and vengeful, too. Since they broke up, the two of them – Esmée and that poisonous little cat she runs with – have made Bryana's life a total misery. She needs somebody like you, a strong arm, to guide and protect her."

"Really?" I raised a questioning brow.

Oh!" Sasha clapped a hand over her mouth. "Am I reading this wrong?

"It's very early days, but no…I wouldn't say you're mistaken in making that assumption."

"Whew!" Sasha wiped her brow. "In that case you'd better start looking for her. You'll need my help to search, this place is a damned rabbit warren on all levels."

Sasha called to a colleague to watch her place. We started with the basement. The dungeon itself, being open plan, it didn't offer many places to hide. We also drew a blank with the basement restroom, plus the one upstairs by the bar, and the locker room.

"Where to next?"

Sasha indicated the wide staircase.

"What's up there?" The sumptuous red, black and gilt décor made it look like the set from a nineteen forties movie. I almost expected to see Ginger Rogers descending on the arm of Fred Astaire prior to one of their famous dance routines.

"The upper floors house all the individual cells. Members rent them, as one would a hotel room, for private play. Wait here, I'll need to grab a pass key." She darted away then returned a few moments later, patting her skimpy shorts. We ascended the stairs side by side and checked the first corridor. Just as I'd expected, the individual rooms on the first level were well appointed with lavish en suite facilities and kitted out for different types of play. A nice setup for those who could afford to pay for the luxury.

We moved on to the next area. "Is there any CCTV in this place?" I asked, now increasingly worried by the negative results.

"Yes, there is, but I'm reluctant to involve the management at this stage." Sasha glanced up at the ceiling then took my arm and pulled me into an alcove. "We've got new owners now and things are not... let's just say I'm not confident the cameras are being used solely for safety and security."

"You mean..." I dropped my voice to match Sasha's whisper .

"I've heard a few rumors that some of our more prominent members have received blackmail threats. I'm not in a position to confirm those rumors or the source of the threats but…"

"Holy cow!" I wanted to get out of here smartish but not without Bryana. My business and the famous guests who flocked to Auchtercairn relied on my ability to offer total confidentiality. Any sniff of sexual indiscretion would have a hoard of paparazzi camping on my doorstep in hours. I couldn't afford to have my good name besmirched and my life raked over by some grubby ratbag journalist, or worse still be forced to pay a premium for the privilege of keeping my name out of the gossip columns.

"Come on." Sasha took my arm and we started on the next group of cells. All but one of them were unoccupied. We moved on swiftly from that one, leaving a startled couple to no doubt wonder who we were and how we had managed to interrupt their private scene. Up another flight of stairs, the cells were smaller, and more basic, yet still functional and all vacant.

"Where to now?"

Sasha shrugged. "That's it, there isn't anywhere else except…" She frowned and shook her head. "No."

"Except where?" I grabbed her by the arms and shook her. "You're wasting valuable time. If you know something, anything, you must tell me."

"In the basement dungeon there's a secret door. A casual observer wouldn't even know it was there; it doesn't lead anywhere except a disused storeroom but, rumor has it, there also used to be a tunnel out to the Heath."

"Come on." I took off at speed leaving Sasha to follow. Back in the basement dungeon, I found things hotting up with quite a few more people either using the equipment or just watching. I masqueraded as a casual observer while I got my breath back and scanned the walls frustrated by the lack of any door. The red spotlights, arranged to play upon the equipment, also cast deep shadows and changed perceptions of space. Sasha eventually reached my side and steered me toward a dimly lit area next to the wheel. Not until I was right up to the wall did I see a faint crack between the stones. I pushed hard but nothing happened. I turned to Sasha and growled angrily, "How does it open?"

Sasha reached around me and pressed a small stone some eight inches from the crack. The door opened inward with barely a sound, to reveal a large space cluttered with broken equipment and discarded furniture. She pushed me inside and flicked a light switch. "Go and search for her," she whispered. "Good luck. I have to return to work now. I'll try to come back for you later."

The door closed and I was on my own. I took my time, moving things, making sure I didn't miss her and I was glad that I did. Bryana was in the far corner, hidden behind a long velvet curtain, both blindfolded and gagged with all four limbs tied to a discarded cross.

"Oh, Bryana, honey. You're safe now." I quickly tore the gag from her mouth and then removed the blindfold. Tears overflowed from her eyes and ran down her cheeks. She moistened her lips with the tip of her tongue but clearly couldn't speak, yet. Then I concentrated on the bindings at her wrists and ankles. It pained me to see how the rough packing twine was cutting into her flesh but I couldn't hurry the process as the knots were really tight and complicated – not the quick release twist knots I used in rope play. Whoever had tied Bryana up didn't mean her to escape. Once Bryana was free, I picked her up, carried her to a long couch and held her tight. "Who did this to you?" I already had a pretty good idea.

Bryana shook her head. "I'm not sure. I didn't actually see them." She shuddered and snuggled closer. "It was over before I had time to blink. One minute, I was standing talking with you and Sasha then the next I was whisked away…there were two of them, both female, I think. The blindfold and gag were simultaneous. Then they dragged me in here and…" Her hand went to her neck. "They took my collar." Her voice broke.

"It doesn't matter, we can get another one made up." I soothed her sobs and cursed the bitches.

"But it won't be the same."

She had a point. The significance of her acceptance had been lost. However, I wasn't going to agree with her.

"Yes it will. The new one will be identical. We will have a little collaring ceremony and make it special."

"I'd like that." Bryana gave a ragged sigh then glanced at the jumbled mess surrounding us. "Where are we?"

"In a storeroom just off the dungeon. Sasha helped me to get in here through a secret door. She put herself on the line helping me to find you but she had to get back to work before she was missed."

"Sasha is a good friend." Bryana's lips twitched in a weak smile. "I want to go home."

I stroked her hair. "And so you shall, my sweet, as soon as I can get us both safely out of here."

"What do you mean?" Bryana jerked away from me, her question uttered as a shrill squeak of alarm.

I took a deep breath before committing myself. "I'm not sure how the door opens from this side. Sasha did say she'd come back for us later, when she could, but I have another idea…" I sent up a silent prayer that it wasn't a wild goose chase. "Sasha also mentioned that there may be another exit, one that leads out onto the Heath. Are you game to give it a try?"

Bryana nodded. "Yes, anything to get away from here without… I never want to set foot inside that dungeon again."

"Right." I stood and offered her my arm. "Let's see if we can find a way out of here and defy your abductors."

Meeting of Minds

Cassie

*Can Cassie find a way forward or is this the
end for her and Bryana?*

$\mathbf{B}$ryana clung onto my arm like a limpet to a rock. "Cassie, are you sure there is another way out of here?" Her brow creased in frown as she surveyed the almost impossible task ahead of us.

After her recent ordeal, I wasn't surprised that she seemed unwilling to lose contact with me even for a second. On top of being tied up, blindfold, and gagged, all without her consent, she'd suffered the indignity of being dumped like a piece of trash in this claustrophobic basement.

I understood her concern and, to be absolutely honest, I also shared her doubts – although I wasn't about to voice them. One of us had to remain strong, and positive. We'd already spent nearly half an hour searching for a way out of this hell-hole – a viable alternative to using the more conventional exit through the club on the other side of the wall.

The vast underground complex was hot, airless, and incredibly cluttered with the detritus of many years scattered everywhere one looked. The vaulted ceiling and supporting foundation walls created a series of arched recesses the size of small rooms that divided the perimeter into separate sections. I recognized the arrangement as similar to the cellars at Auchtercairn which had originally been intended to store wines, spirits, and other essential supplies to provide for the occupants above. Although every one of these bays was now crammed with discarded furniture and broken equipment from the dungeon whilst the central area seemed to have become a dumping ground for cartons and packaging material. It wasn't easy to see any of the walls or work out where an exit might be hidden.

So far, we'd drawn a blank with the sections on one long wall – to the right of the door – and the second set of bays to the left side didn't appear very promising either.

"Sasha was pretty confident there was." I gave Bryana an encouraging smile and we moved on a few paces, checking every foot of wall for anything that looked like a way out. "Apparently this old mansion has been a venue for all kinds of vice since early Victorian times. She told me that the hidden exit has been in use since then to enable guests to evade the frequent vice squad raids, as well as irate fathers searching for their wayward daughters."

"Oh, I didn't know that..." Bryana sighed and tightened her grip on my arm. I could feel the tension in her fingers where they dug into my flesh. Her gaze flitted around the area where we now stood surrounded by piles of discarded divans and drapes before returning to me. "Please tell me we'll find the way out soon, I'm scared...scared that they'll come back and carry out their threats to..." Her voice tailed off as if she couldn't bring herself to say what was uppermost in her mind. She shuddered. The action brought her closer to me and I wrapped my arms around her.

"I know... Don't fret, you're safe with me. Those women won't stand a chance if they come back." I held her tight, fitting her curves against my body, and kissed her forehead. "You need to be brave for just a little longer. I'll get us out of here in no time." My promise carried more faith than hope. I hated to admit defeat in anything, and especially in this instance, since I wanted to prove my invincibility in Bryana's eyes. Defeat also meant going back through the club, and neither of us wanted to do that. Bryana, because she was scared witless after being snatched from under my nose, stripped of her collar, and imprisoned in this shit hole. Although she hadn't identified the women involved I'd be willing to bet my entire fortune that the culprits were those sick bitches Esmée Vincent and, her poisonous sidekick, Marisa. Whilst I, based on Sasha's information which I had no reason to doubt, couldn't afford to lay myself open to blackmail by the criminals who now apparently controlled Out of Bounds. Thankfully Bryana had signed me in as her guest, so my name wasn't in the book, but my face was too well known for comfort, and my family connections put me in a very vulnerable position. I'd be in deep shit if the press got hold of my name and forged a link between this club and my activities at Auchtercairn.

Besides all of the above, however, I desperately wanted, needed, Bryana to acknowledge my strength and regard me as her knight in shining armor. To have her turn automatically to me in times of stress and look on me as protector, lover, and Mistress. It was a big ask. To achieve all of the above, I must first demonstrate my ability to solve our current dilemma and prove that I was the ultimate safe haven.

More determined than ever to find a way out of this crap hole, I released Bryana from my embrace, took her by the hand, and pressed on with the search. A couple of flickering strip lights provided barely enough illumination to penetrate the gloom behind a row of cartons lined up close to the third wall. I'd almost given up the hunt when I came across an anomaly.

Had I been a casual observer I probably wouldn't have noticed how what looked like a haphazard jumble of larger cartons had been cleverly arranged so they formed a ragged barrier blocking off the view of one complete bay. I pushed into a narrow gap between two of the taller cartons, dragging Bryana in my wake, and discovered an L-shaped passage at the end of which, hung a large curtain, similar to the one used to cover

Bryana. The dark velvet drape reached from the ceiling to floor and spanned an entire arched section.

What purpose would a curtain serve in a windowless cellar?

The answer was self-evident when I pulled the heavy fabric aside to reveal a hidden area almost a small room in size and completely empty of clutter. Somebody had taken a lot of trouble to keep this space hidden from general view. I estimated that twenty or thirty people could hide in here and nobody would be the wiser.

"Oh!" Bryana voiced her surprise at first sight of the solid looking door set in the back wall.

I had to admit the door looked promising but knew I mustn't get my hopes up too soon; it could just as easily lead nowhere. Although why anybody would want to disguise the entrance to a cupboard, or even another room was beyond me. I shrugged off a wave of negative thoughts, refusing to consider defeat or even having to repeat the search process elsewhere. I stepped forward and tried the handle. The door opened smoothly on well oiled hinges to reveal a narrow passage. I peered into the gloom. Elation and fear in equal measure clenched my stomach into a tight knot.

Light! We needed light to navigate our way out of here. My heart beat a rapid paradiddle of frustration laced with anticipation as I felt around the entrance for a switch. Eventually I found a time delay push-button, like the ones you get on staircases. A trial depression produced a series of dim globes that snaked away into the distance and provided a feeble but adequate illumination.

"Yes!" Bryana surged forward almost taking me with her. "Let's get out of here."

"Wait! We can't go yet." I dug my heels in, halting her over eager charge for freedom, and wedged the door open with my hip. I wasn't prepared to risk the unknown until I figured out how much time we had before the lights went out. Getting stuck in an unlit passage that led nowhere spelt disaster in my book.

The passage was suddenly plunged into darkness again.

"Oh!" Bryana gave an audible gasp and sought closer contact with my body. I wrapped my arms around her waist, drawing her against me for a moment.

It had taken a bare ninety seconds, by my reckoning, which meant we didn't have much time to reach, find, and depress, the next switch assuming there was one.

I steered Bryana back into the storeroom and the door, obviously controlled by a strong spring, closed with a soft clunk. There were a couple more things I needed to do before we took our chance on the passage. I turned my attention to Bryana. "Have you got a lipstick?"

She nodded, frowning, no doubt puzzled by my strange request, although she unhooked her purse from her belt and passed it over without question. As a fully paid-up femme, I imagine, Bryana never went anywhere without lipstick. I extracted the gilt tube then tore a flap of cardboard from one of the large cartons that made up the wall, scrawled a brief message in bold, bright red, lettering *"B safe. Will call U later. C."* I didn't want Sasha to worry if she managed to come back to look for us when she got her break. There was no guarantee she would get the chance, it depended on how busy the dungeon became or even who was manning the CCTV covering that area. From what she'd said, and subtly hinted too, I gathered a close watch was kept on activities both upstairs, in the private cells as well as the public areas, and down in the communal dungeon.

Bryana gave me a weak smile when I handed back her purse. She hung onto my sleeve, keeping close, as I made my way back to the main area and propped the message up facing the other entrance.

On our way back to the hidden passage, I collected a couple of metal struts from a pile of trashed dungeon equipment. One to wedge the door ajar in case we needed to retrace our steps – since from what I'd seen it didn't have a handle on the inside – and the other to carry as insurance. I believed in being prepared for any eventuality, however bizarre the idea may be.

"Right, are you ready?" I opened the door and set one metal strut on the floor to stop it from closing completely then waited for Bryana's nod of assent before I hit the timer button, but it didn't come.

Bryana shook her head and even in the half light I read a look of deep anxiety in her eyes. "No, I just thought of something. What…" Her voice cracked. "What if we meet somebody coming the other way?"

"Very unlikely. Besides I have this." I waved the second metal bar to reassure her. "My guess is this exit is one way only, an emergency escape that locks automatically to prevent unauthorized access. Did you see what happened when we stepped away from the door?"

"Oh, I didn't think of that." Bryana relaxed visibly, seemingly happy to accept my reassurance. "I'm ready now."

I said a silent prayer, for a blessing from Lady Luck, then pressed the timer and the lights came on. "Let's go!" I urged her. "Hold onto my arm and keep moving no matter what happens. I have no idea how far away the next light switch is, or the exit for that matter. We just have to walk fast and hope we get there in time."

The exit turned out to be quite a distance away, much farther than I'd expected. Three more sections of lights awaited and, despite the unpleasant impression of walls pressing in on us, I paused to time-test each one before venturing into the unknown. We emerged into fresh night air from what appeared to be a non-descript storm drain. The muffled clang of the iron grill as it shut behind us was music to my ears. Before we moved away from the spot I posted the metal strut back through the grill. I didn't want to get nabbed by the police for carrying a lethal weapon.

"Where are we?" Bryana shivered against me, her teeth chattering, despite a warm breeze that rustled softly through the leaves of the clump of trees enclosing the small open space where we stood.

Good question.

"I'm not entirely sure." I looked around trying to get my bearings, waiting for my eyes to adjust to the lack of light. With the sky way too cloudy for moonlight to play a part, we were enveloped in a cocoon of darkness. Although we certainly weren't miles from anywhere nor isolated in the heart of the countryside. Hampstead Heath was an oasis of green space in the heart of a big city bordered by the adjacent densely populated suburbs of Highgate and Golders Green to the north with Camden, Westminster and the City of London to the south. However, the reflected amber glow of distant street lighting merely accentuated the depth of shadow out here on the Heath.

"We're not that far from a road. See..." I pointed through a small gap in the trees toward an arc of light in the night sky. Although several hundred yards away, seeing the vehicle's headlights gave me fresh hope. Based on the location of the club plus the distance we'd walked along that passage, I guessed it was Spaniards Road or even better North End Way. Either road promised a cruising black cab and safe transport back to Docklands. No point in me wishing for the moon and the means to call for a pick-up though, in accordance with the club's strict 'no cell phones' policy, we had both left ours back at the apartment. Now, of course, I was glad that we'd done so or our phones would still be languishing in a locked box at the reception desk. I shuddered at the thought. Thankful that foresight had saved me the bother of having to front up at the club tomorrow to retrieve them and the potential risk of being asked to show identity or explain our unorthodox exit. I'd had one lucky escape from that nightmare scenario, and another in finding the way out of the club. Now I just needed a final bit of good fortune to get us both home safely.

"Come on." I took Bryana's hand and started walking briskly toward the road but after a just few paces, she stumbled and nearly fell. "Hey! Watch your step." I placed a steadying arm around her waist then pulled her close and silenced her sobs with a soft kiss. Bryana relaxed against me. For a moment I forgot where we were and drowned in the pleasure of her lips, so sweet, so tempting. Her proximity and the heightened tension of the whole episode had awakened a sleeping dragon that now breathed the fire of lust into my body. It was a small step in my mind to make use of our secluded position and the soft bed of leaves. No, with some reluctance, I forced myself to resist the urge to pursue that action and put her from me. This was neither the time nor the place for such thoughts, however much my body screamed for satisfaction. We needed to get to the road in one piece, no mean feat when it meant negotiating a tract of rough terrain in the darkness, and then find a cab ride back to her apartment.

"Are you okay to go on now?"

"Yes." Bryana clutched my arm tighter, her sniffles fading.

"Good." Using the intermittent flash of vehicle headlights as a guide, I started forward again, encouraging her into to follow my lead. Although, being forced to temper my naturally long stride and rapid pace to accommodate her heels meant our progress was painfully slow. From time to time I almost lost confidence when a vehicle passed by on the distant road and it seemed we weren't making any headway. I had to keep reminding myself that every step, however small, brought us closer to our goal.

Our nightmare evening finally ground to a close when the cab pulled up outside Bryana's apartment block shortly after three thirty in the morning. The walk across the Heath had taken much longer than I expected then the wait for an empty cab to come along had compounded things. I shook Bryana who was dozing with her head on my shoulder. "We're home, honey."

"What!" She jerked away from me, clearly alarmed by the suddenness of her awakening.

We extricated ourselves from the vehicle and I paid the fare, adding a hefty tip in gratitude to the driver for coming all the way out to Docklands at this hour. Bryana sagged against me, clearly exhausted by the night's traumatic events; I put my arm about her waist for support and led her inside to the elevator.

Once inside her seventh floor apartment I steered Bryana toward my room. It had become a given for her to sleep in my bed, not that we'd done much sleeping the last few nights. Between talking, exploring our compatibility and the early stages of what might in time become a fully fledged D/s relationship, plus some very satisfying sexual marathons, sleep didn't stand much chance.

At the door, she suddenly roused from her lethargy and tried to pull away from me "No, I can't...I want to be alone."

"Are you sure?" I'd have thought being alone tonight was the last thing she'd have wanted. I didn't understand her propensity for isolation rather than sharing. The concept went against my natural instinct which was to take care of her, to provide the comfort and security to soothe away all her fears, but it was her choice. I couldn't force her into staying with me if she wanted to be alone.

"Yes..." Bryana shuddered and cast her gaze to the floor. "After what happened tonight I feel dirty and I can't bear for you to look at me or touch me."

"Okay, whatever makes you happy." I didn't understand her position but I changed direction toward her room and stopped at the door. "I want you to know I'm here if you need me for anything."

"Thanks, Cassie."

Bryana refused to meet my gaze, though I recognized the note of relief in her voice. I released her, opened the door and stood back so she could enter. "Sleep tight. We'll talk tomorrow when you feel better." She didn't respond but simply moved into the room and closed the door firmly in my face.

Needless to say, I couldn't sleep. The hubbub in my brain refused to quieten down. Instead I processed the night's events, examining them endlessly from every angle, trying to figure out why Esmée would want to torture Bryana. Was it revenge – for Bryana looking elsewhere, jealousy, or something more sinister? Revenge didn't seem in any way logical, since Bryana hadn't even formed a new relationship when the reign of terror started. Besides which, Esmée had a new love interest and a new sub to dominate. Jealousy? Maybe, but unlikely, I mentally shook my head. The more sinister explanation, however, made perfect sense to me. A case of: *'even though we're not together any more I still want to control you and, if I can't keep you under my thumb, I'll mess with your head to make damned sure nobody else can have you'*. Marisa's role in this little drama was easily explained. She probably just did as she was told, seizing upon the chance to please her Mistress while loving every minute of being allowed to torment her lover's ex.

I would need to work extra hard to break the hold that Esmée still had over Bryana's mind. My desire to help Bryana free herself from the clutches of these two women wasn't entirely selfish, to serve my own ends, but because what I'd both seen and heard of Esmée had convinced me she wasn't a safe person to be around. She didn't care enough to give a novice sub what she needed most; a safe environment to develop both physically and, more importantly, intellectually. I hated to think she was practicing her particular brand of mind control and domination without any proper knowledge of, or dedication to, the lifestyle. Bryana was a mess because of Esmée. I aimed to put that right if I could, and the sooner the better.

Just over an hour later, much earlier than I'd anticipated, Bryana's screams rent through the silent apartment. I was out of bed and racing for her room within seconds. Her tormented cry for help gave me the perfect opportunity to prove myself the hero in her eyes. She was sitting up amid a tangle of bedclothes that spoke of her disturbed sleep. The look of fear on her face melted my heart.

"Come here." I wrapped my arms around her and held her close. The rapid beat of her heart kept up a steady rhythm against my chest. "Want to tell me what's wrong?"

"I…I don't know, I can't remember." Cassie pulled free of me. She retreated across the bed, out of reach, and chewed on her lip. "I think I had another bad dream. I've had a lot of them lately."

Her reluctant admission set off a chain reaction. Tears flowed from troubled eyes in a seemingly unstoppable cascade. Then she began to tremble, her body visibly shaking and her teeth chattering. I could only guess at who and what had provoked this event. It bugged me that she wouldn't, or couldn't, trust me or even let me close enough to admit her fears. Until she did, I couldn't really help her overcome the trauma. I wanted to show her I could be her rock, her confidant and her Mistress all rolled into one. That she could get the relief she craved by unburdening her fears, and the tension they created, onto my shoulders either in words or actions. If, as she claimed, she felt dirty, I had the perfect answer for that, too. Over the years, working with other tortured souls, I'd developed a foolproof technique that combined deep massage and verbal expression to cleanse both mind and body of all the unnecessary baggage left from previous abusive or destructively unhealthy relationships. It was proven to work but the subject had to place their trust in me first.

Eventually Bryana relented and allowed me to get close enough to comfort her although it took nearly an hour before she relaxed enough to drift off into exhausted sleep. I stayed with her the remainder of the night, holding her close, stroking her beautiful hair and reveling in her soft fragrant body resting against my chest. It took a massive amount of willpower on my part to resist the call of my libido. To me it seemed wrong to be this close and yet not to touch her or taste her. However, I didn't want to do anything that would alienate Bryana or destroy the fragile trust she'd placed in me.

The following few days passed quietly, and without any incident of note. To be on the safe side, I deliberately kept away from sensitive subjects for fear of initiating an adverse reaction. Outwardly, Bryana had returned to her normal self but I sensed that she still harbored many fears and doubts on the inside. She worked long hours each day meticulously checking the equipment for her upcoming trip. I was amazed by the plethora of cameras, lenses and filters that she needed, even in this digital age. It didn't end with the equipment. There were endless phone calls, plus reams of paperwork, shooting plans, and permits littering the desk in her office, all of which formed a necessary part of her job. Being a successful fashion photographer clearly required a lot of hard work and forward planning.

Although away from home and my office, I was able to keep up with most work on the laptop. My business activities generated a steady stream of correspondence, invoices to check and bills to pay but I often stopped to watch Bryana. I got a kick out of seeing her working so hard at the preparation and that set me wondering about the other side, the actual fashion shoots. In the past, I'd been present during both photo and video sessions in the dungeon. Was fashion much different? Maybe Bryana would let me watch her in action? A trip to Amsterdam with her would be a perfect way to develop our relationship.

"Why do you want to come with me?" Bryana rounded angrily upon me following the suggestion that I might accompany her. "Don't you trust me?"

Interesting reaction.

That she put lack of trust at the top of her list told me a lot about her relationship with Esmée.

"It's not a matter of trust." Disappointment sat heavily in my gut like an indigestible meal. "Have you even considered the fact that I might want to come to Amsterdam with you because I both love your company and a few days away together will be an exciting adventure?" It annoyed and saddened me that Bryana let paranoia control her life at every turn. Worse still, that Esmée haunted our relationship like a ghost, her evil presence stamping out any positive progress before it had a chance to take root let alone grow new shoots. I found it totally frustrating when everything I suggested or asked of Bryana, even something that she might enjoy, received a negative or obstructive response. As long as Esmée's pernicious influence prevailed Bryana was reluctant to face life head on.

"I'm going there to work, not to play."

I shook my head at Bryana's stonewall answer saddened that she still didn't get where I was coming from.

"Of course you are, and I wouldn't dream of interfering with that part of your day." *Except perhaps to watch from a distance.* "I just thought you might like some company when you're not working." There wasn't any point in me adding 'and some protection from the likes of Esmée and Marisa' since I didn't want to poke a stick into that particular wasp's nest. Besides, I didn't even know if either of them would be in Amsterdam. I understood, from the little information Bryana had shared with me, that this wasn't a big public fashion show like those in Paris or Rome but some sort of upmarket catalog shoot. Her remit from Célestin Reynaud, the designer, involved using many of Amsterdam's famous landmarks, buildings, canals, and tourist sites as a backdrop for the collection. However I didn't want to take any risks. There was every chance that Marisa might be one of the models, and where Marisa went Esmée would be sure to follow – especially if she'd got wind of Bryana's involvement. "We could take a leisurely dinner cruise on the canal, visit a few nightclubs, even try our hand at the casino, or just relax and unwind. It's been a rough few days for both of us."

"Yes...It has. I...I'm..." Bryana twisted her hands together and refused to meet my gaze.

"What do you think?" Without thinking, my hand automatically rested on her shoulder. "Shall I book myself a seat on the plane?"

"No!" Bryana dodged away from my hand, moved out of reach, and strode across the room.

Her emphatic response left me totally baffled. She spent several long minutes staring out the window – I doubt, however, she was admiring the view of the Thames – before she turned back to me her face set in an inscrutable mask. "I can't do this anymore... It's over... I want you to leave. Now!"

"But–" The suddenness of this bombshell robbed me of speech. What had changed? Bryana appeared to have forgotten our original agreement that I could stay until she left for Amsterdam on Monday at which time we'd review the arrangement.

Bryana glared at me. "No buts! Frankly I don't care where you go. I just want you out of my face. Today!"

Hells bells! My normally submissive Bryana had morphed into a tiger, one not shy about displaying teeth and claws, either. She needed a gentle reminder that I wasn't the bad guy here. However, her unequivocal dismissal left me precious little room for maneuver.

I resorted to humor in an attempt to defuse the tension. "You're a hard woman, turning me out onto the streets when you know I'm homeless for at least the next six weeks and maybe a couple more."

Although technically I would never be homeless, even though Auchtercairn was temporarily full of strangers, I could always return to my apartment. However, Bryana didn't know that I kept a one bedroom pied-a-terre in the apartment block in Curzon Street. I always avoided telling people that I owned property in fashionable Mayfair; it gave them a totally wrong impression of my financial status. I'd inherited Auchtercairn, the family estate, from my father, along with several other properties in London and elsewhere. The houses and apartment blocks, however, amounted to nothing more than white elephants since all the income from rents was swallowed up in maintenance and taxes.

"It's not my concern if you're homeless, or that damned castle of yours is occupied by a film crew. You'll survive. Women like you always do."

I ignored the 'women like you' jibe and offered a conciliatory comment in an attempt to win her around. "Maybe I will...but it won't be the same without you."

"Rubbish! You don't care a fuck what happens to me – this is all about you. You want to control me...to manipulate me for you own sick pleasure, just like Esmée did. Well, I've had enough."

Ouch! I couldn't believe what I was hearing. Bryana had seriously lost the plot. "You have a very short memory. Surely, if I didn't care, I'd have left you to rot in that stinking cellar."

"Not if it served your own ends."

Again, ouch! The knife found its mark in my chest, sliding easily between my ribs and wounding my heart. "That is not fair. You speak as though I have a hidden agenda, or some devious plan to hurt you, when nothing could be further from the truth. I just want to help you...to free you from the hurt and fear that Esmée planted in your mind which is now holding you hostage." What else could I say to make Bryana understand? I certainly wasn't likely to get very far by trading insults and raised voices.

Bryana's outburst proved beyond doubt that like a lot of people, even novice subs, she had a distorted view of the lifestyle. She clearly knew, or understood, very little about how a true D/s relationship worked for those involved. Had she never learnt anything about the mutual love, trust, and willingness to serve that inextricably binds Mistress and sub together? I'd hoped that, with the right guidance, she might fully understand and want to explore the possibilities of building that sort of bond with me.

"You are not listening to me." Bryana stared me down. "I told you to get out!"

I sighed. Sadly, it didn't look like I was going to get the chance to show her how a good D/s contract could change her life or offer her the happy ending she deserved. I gave it one more shot. "It breaks my heart to leave you when you're so troubled."

"See if I care." She shrugged and started to turn away, leaving me none the wiser what was going through her mind.

Incensed by her intractable attitude, my patience snapped. I reached for her arm and spun her around to face me.

"Don't walk away from me!" I pulled her closer, making sure I had her attention. "It's time you stopped this nonsense and started communicating like an adult."

Her lips parted but no words emerged, just a hiss of breath that brushed my cheek like a silky zephyr. I couldn't help myself; it had been too long since we were this close. I dipped my head, smothering Bryana's protest as I sealed our lips together in a kiss. She struggled to free herself but I held her tight until she stilled and finally capitulated, melting into my embrace.

Satisfied I'd achieved a small victory; I broke the kiss and held her gaze. My heart raced in my chest. I couldn't breathe. This was make or break time. If I failed to clear this important hurdle our relationship really would be over. I sucked air into my starved lungs.

"We need to talk. Sensibly, like the adults we are. Cards on the table." There was so much more I wanted to say but didn't for fear it would tip her into another tantrum. Tension gripped my chest until it felt like it was being compressed in a vice, and Bryana had full control of the bar.

The silence lengthened. I remained still, waiting for some sign from Bryana who appeared to be doing battle with her inner demons.

She eventually came out of her trance-like state and a heavy sigh escaped her lips. "Very well. We can talk, if you insist." Her reluctant agreement was heavily laced with the inference that talking would do us, or more specifically me, little good.

Having agreed to my request Bryana broke eye contact and I sensed her physically withdrawing from me. To change the focus, I took her wrist and led her to the white leather couch. The starkness of the minimalistic, black and white décor gave the room an impersonal feel that took some getting used to after the warmth of Auchtercairn with its clutter of antique furniture, pictures, and carpets.

"Look at me." I kept a firm hold of her for fear she would simply get up and walk away from me if I didn't restrain her and focus her attention. "Despite what you've said,and erroneously believe, I do care about you – very much – and I also care what happens to our relationship. Yes, I know you're hurting badly, I can see it in your eyes and your body language, but I can make all that hurt go away, if you'll let me."

Bryana shook her head.

Her mute denial made me all the more determined to show her there was a way out of the mental chaos that was preventing her from leading a normal life. Her gaze drifted away from me.

I hooked one finger under her chin and forced her to face me. "Let me in. Make me understand where you're coming from. Tell me what you're thinking and feeling. What you need to heal the wounds both mental and physical. Come on, Bryana, trust me. I can make all the bad things go away." I hoped, once I got her talking about her fears, it would prove cathartic and everything would fall into place.

Bryana's eyes widened. "I can't. I..."

"Yes you can. Let it all out and you'll feel a lot better."

"No..." She sagged against me, the tension dropping away from her body along with the tears soaking my shoulder.

Frustrating though it was to restrain my natural impulse I was determined to take things slowly until she was fully back to some semblance of normality.

The main problem we faced was that our relationship had begun in the wrong place, at the wrong point, and to a large extent with misconceptions on both sides – certainly on mine. From our first encounter, Bryana had presented herself, as more experienced and well-versed in the lifestyle than she actually was. The past few weeks had shown me the fallacy of that assumption. Bryana's relationship with Esmée, and her visits to Out Of Bounds, had merely served to confuse rather than educate. My task, if our relationship survived beyond today, would be to undo all the damage and make her whole again. A necessary stage before we could build a future based on openness, truth, and understanding. I hoped we still had enough going for us to work out a proper contract, one that would give Bryana the confidence to embark on a journey of discovery. I was certain, with the right training, she could, and would, blossom into the perfect sub for me.

When I judged her tears were easing, I tried again. "Talk to me, Bryana. Tell me everything."

"A little, maybe, if you're sure." Bryana raised her head and met my gaze. She dabbed at the tears still misting her beautiful sapphire blue eyes. "You really don't want me to burden you with all the gory details."

"Yes, I do," I tightened my hand over her wrist. "That's the whole point; for you to talk it all out of your system."

Bryana sighed. "That will take more time than you or I can spare right now." She glanced at her watch. Goodness me, it's gone three o'clock and I haven't prepared any lunch. I must feed you first and then maybe we can talk for a while."

Somewhat uncharitably, I accused her of employing delaying tactics. However, a break for a meal and a glass or two of wine might provide a platform free of tension. With Bryana in a relaxed frame of mind there was every chance we might make a little progress toward a resolution.

We adjourned to the kitchen area in search of food. Bryana refused my help, saying she could manage.

However, after she'd spent several minutes immobile, just staring into the fridge, it was clear her optimism was misplaced. Eventually, she closed the fridge door and turned around, eyes downcast, her face troubled. "I'm sorry, Cassie, there isn't much here, not enough for a proper meal anyway, I'll have to go..."

I stepped forward. "Let me see."

Bryana cringed away from me, real fear showing on her face. Hell! Did she imagine that I would beat her because there wasn't enough food? Is that the sort of treatment Esmée meted out on a regular basis? My blood ran cold at the thought. I delved into the fridge and came up with a few mushrooms, half a red bell pepper, a zucchini, and some pecorino Romano cheese. The cupboard yielded rice, a tin of sweet corn, olive oil, and a stock cube. She was right, it wasn't a lot, but plenty to make a meal for the two of us with bread and wine. I set to work and in a little over thirty minutes we were enjoying the fruits of my labors.

"That was really good." Bryana laid her fork down and wiped the plate clean with a piece of bread. "I'd never have thought to turn those few odd bits into a tasty risotto." She popped the bread into her mouth.

"Thank you, honey." I smiled, accepting her praise although I hadn't really done that much. The tip of her tongue swept across her lips, to gather up an errant crumb and my imagination immediately flicked into another place. The thought of that soft pink organ caressing my body sent rampant desire racing through me. More importantly though, I really wanted to rekindle the cozy intimacy we'd lost – that Esmée's cruel intervention had snatched away. Just little things really, but I missed them so badly: a stolen kiss, a fleeting touch that set my skin alive with goose bumps, a secret smile that said 'I can't wait to get you alone and rip your clothes off', all those things and more gave our relationship substance.

"May I make some coffee?"

Bryana's question floored me for a moment. Before I realized that in the last few days, since her ordeal at the club, she'd changed. Now she always either asked permission to do something simple, like making a drink, or apologized for not providing whatever in a timely manner. Then today, for the first time, Bryana had shown a brief flash of backbone, and outrage, at the treatment meted out by Esmée. Maybe the healing process had begun. I sincerely hoped that was the case.

"Coffee would be good." I rose and began to collect the dishes but Bryana shooed me away. "You cooked, I'll clear up. Go and sit down. I'll serve coffee in a little while."

Good as her word, less than ten minutes elapsed before Bryana carried a tray with coffee, my favorite malt whisky, and a dish of amaretto biscuits over to the seating area.

We spent the remainder of the day and the entire weekend in relative harmony. Outwardly relaxed, we chatted about this and that, but to my dismay hardly touched on anything important. Somehow, in all that time, Bryana managed to avoid talking in depth about her personal feelings, hopes and fears. Every time we got too close to the things that troubled her she steered the conversation away to another topic. Although, she did relent on one point – that I could accompany her to Amsterdam, for which I was mightily relieved. Once I'd secured her agreement, I wasted no time in getting my airline ticket booked, before she could change her mind.

Monday morning found us too busy to let anything intrude on a multitude of last minute must-do jobs. Before we had time to blink, or think, the taxi arrived to carry us to London City airport for the flight to Amsterdam. As the day progressed, however, Bryana grew quieter, and more introspective.

By the time we landed at Schiphol airport early in the afternoon, she'd drifted away from me again, retreating into her own space, a place where I wasn't welcome. As EU citizens we passed smoothly through the automated immigration channel and took the fast train into Amsterdam Centraal. The walk to our hotel, situated near the old Kirk and only a few hundred yards from station, took less than ten minutes.

My basic needs saw me unpacked in record time. I sat by the window in our room waiting, watching, while

Bryana dealt with more cosmetics, clothes and shoes than the average woman would need for a month let alone four days. I waited until she put the last item away before I spoke. "How about a stroll along the canal?"

"I can't." Without a pause to consider my suggestion, Bryana humped her aluminum equipment bag onto her bed, manipulated the combination lock, and threw open the lid. "I need to sort this lot out and then get ready to meet Célestin and the crew for working dinner."

"That's not for hours yet." I crossed the room and pulled her hand away from the bag. "You can do that later. A little exercise, some fresh air, and a light snack will do us both good."

"I suppose so." Bryana glanced longingly at her cameras and other equipment then back to me. "Maybe just a short break."

Bryana's reluctance to relax drove me to distraction. It was as if she feared the world would come crashing down about her ears if she stopped working for a second. Maybe it would. I considered the possibility that her incessant need to work kept her sane. Being busy meant she didn't have to face up to reality.

"Okay, let's go." I took her arm and started toward the door before she could change her mind.

"Hang on a minute, if we're going to walk far I must change my shoes." Bryana pulled free and swapped the heeled platform pumps in which she'd travelled for a pair of equally high black strappy, gladiator style, sandals that buckled right up around the ankle. Then she paused at the vanity unit to check her appearance, renew her lip gloss, and run a brush over her already sleek dark blonde hair. Finally satisfied, she grabbed her purse and joined me at the door.

I've always loved this area of old Amsterdam, with its narrow streets, tree lined canals, and quaint architecture. At this time of day it is both beautiful and relatively quiet, but it really comes alive late in the evening when lights shine from many of the windows. Then the quiet thoroughfares transform into the famous Red Light District made up of bars, clubs, and sex establishments that attract tourists from all over the world.

We wandered along the tree-lined Oudezijds Voorburgwal at a leisurely pace until we found a café with outside tables from where we could watch the boats on the canal. Bryana declined to join me in a beer and instead ordered a black coffee to accompany our shared platter of cheese, bread, and tapenade.

"This is so good." Bryana used a piece of bread to capture the last scrape of the olive paste from the small dish. She popped the bread into her mouth, closed her eyes, and made an exaggerated show of savoring the taste. "I have no idea why I even thought I wouldn't like it." A smile flitted across her face. "You are so good for me. I'd never have dared to try this on my own."

I reached for her hand. "Hey, honey, I can be good for you in lots of ways if you'd let me." The words escaped my lips before my brain engaged. Damn! I'd promised myself I wouldn't rush her and here I was at the first opportunity doing just that.

Bryana's fingers intertwined briefly with mine, before she withdrew her hand. A film of moisture clouded her blue eyes. "I know." Her voice was so quiet I almost missed what she said.

My heart jolted. Was this a breakthrough? I wouldn't let myself believe just yet. We'd come a long way in the past few days but had an even longer way to go. I prayed that Bryana would find the courage to open up her mind and explore all the possibilities waiting for her.

Mindful of her need to keep busy, I took the initiative. "Are you ready to go back to the hotel now?"

"Yes, please."

Bryana was out of her seat and ready to move in seconds. For once she didn't shy away from me when I took her hand.

The confines of the hotel elevator brought her closer. The urge to kiss her sweet lips overwhelmed me. Hell, I wanted much more, but a kiss would have to suffice for now. The doors swished open before I could act on my decision. Once inside our room, I trapped her body against the wall and sealed our lips together, smothering her protest.

I couldn't recall how long it was since we'd shared an impromptu intimate moment. My hands swept her body, molding her curves, and I felt her tremble. The sensation destroyed my resolve to take this one step at a time. Fuck! I needed to touch her, taste her, hear my name on her scream of pleasure when she came for me and, most importantly, have her submit to everything willingly with no reservations, no holding back.

The urgency of my need must have communicated itself to Bryana; she didn't resist when I began to undo her top. I tore at recalcitrant buttons anxious to make contact with bare flesh. Finally, the buttons gave way and I spread the two halves of her shirt. My fingers explored delicately perfumed skin and my thumbs teased her breasts, circling the lacy cups that encased them.

"Oh, Cassie." Her chest rose and fell, her breathing rapid.

My name on her lips, accompanied by a soft moan, sounded so good.

With two hands I swept the shirt from her shoulders and down her arms until it fell to the floor. Then I reached for the zipper on her pencil skirt; the teeth parted smoothly allowing the garment to slither down her thighs and pool around her feet. Bryana remained passive, standing before me, her gaze lowered submissively, allowing me to dictate both the sequence and speed of events.

God, the breath caught in my throat. She was so beautiful, so fragile, so incredibly sexy wearing just lace underwear and sheer, barely black, stockings. Just perfect for... I was tempted to fetch the length of rope from my bag, to bind her slender wrists together and haul them up above her head, but that would be going a step too far at this point in time. Although my head immediately filled with images of the white silk cord twisted into intricate knots across her body, binding her securely, and I could almost hear her voice begging me for relief. I dismissed temptation and reached out to lower the straps of her bra which acted like mild constraints in keeping her arms by her side. As the shallow cups dropped down, her breasts spilled from their confines bobbing slightly as they adjusted to freedom. Her nipples stood proud and erect from dark aureoles proclaiming her heightened state.

With the tip of my index finger I traced a line from her throat through the valley between her breasts and down to the diamond stud in her navel. My finger nail left a faint dark line, a momentary blemish on her perfect skin that sent spikes of desire racing through my body to escape as throbbing heat between my thighs. I repeated the process, this time pressing just that bit harder, leaving a second line beside the first which was already fading. Bryana shuddered, her fingers scrabbled against the wall. Her lips parted to expel a soft gasp which I took to be of pleasure. At least I hoped it meant that, since I wanted to pleasure her so badly.

I dropped to my knees and pressed my face to her midriff, dipping my tongue into her navel, before tentatively moving lower to put my mouth over the scrap of black lace that covered her mound.

She was so ready. I could feel her heat, her individual aroma filled my senses and lifted my desire to a new level. My tongue probed the moist fabric of the g-string.

Moment of truth time.

Would Bryana relax enough to let her orgasm build to a climax or would she freeze and slam the door on the relief she so badly needed at the last moment? My fingers spanned her thighs and I used my thumbs to massage the soft flesh close to the apex. She reacted by widening her stance and pushing her pelvis toward me. My tongue slipped past the narrow strip of fabric to probe her slit.

She tasted so sweet. My head swam, the gathering pace of desire driving me on. I slid my tongue across velvety flesh seeking her pleasure point. When my tongue made contact with her clit, Bryana jerked violently and her legs began to tremble. I probed the hardened peak, teasing it gently then building up both speed and pressure.

"Cassie!"

Bryana shouted out my name. I felt the orgasmic force sweep through her body like a tsunami before developing into a series of convulsions that seemed to ripple endlessly. When the tide slowed I stood, scooped her up in my arms and carried her to my bed.

"Oh! Cassie..." Bryana dissolved into tears.

"Don't try to talk." I sealed her lips with a kiss then spooned my body against Bryana's, holding her close until her sobs faded and she drifted off to sleep.

Just before seven o'clock, I escorted Bryana across the lobby of a smart hotel on the Nieuwe Doelenstraat for her working dinner. She turned a lot of heads. The raspberry-red outfit accentuated her curves and her coloring. Toning peep-toe patent pumps, impeccable make-up, matching nail lacquer, and upswept hair completed the picture. I felt so proud having her walk by my side and found it hard to believe that she'd achieved such perfection in barely half an hour. I left her at reception awaiting directions to the meeting room. From her expression when I suggested she call me to collect her at the end of the evening I doubted she would bother.

For my part I explored the immediate area, finding few changes since my last visit. Then I found a quiet place to eat smoked eel, steak with a salad, and indulge my sweet tooth with a delicious chocolate confection.

I returned to our hotel room just before nine o'clock and found a note had been slipped under the door. I opened the folded sheet, realized immediately it was intended for Bryana, and unashamedly read on.

YOU WILL NOT TURN YOUR BACK AND JUST WALK AWAY FROM ME.

REMEMBER OUT OF BOUNDS?

NEXT TIME YOU WON'T ESCAPE.

DON'T EXPECT CASSIE STUART TO PROTECT YOU.

THE STUPID BITCH WILL RUN A MILE RATHER THAN HAVE HER PRECIOUS SECRETS EXPOSED.

I'M WATCHING AND WAITING.

YOU WILL OBEY ME OR SUFFER THE CONSEQUENCES.

My blood ran cold. Somebody clearly meant business. There was no signature but I couldn't imagine the author as anybody other than Esmée Vincent. No mystery that she'd found us, since I'd discovered earlier in the day that this was Bryana's usual hotel. I cursed myself for not realizing the possibility of something like this and taking preventative action. Although how she'd got the hotel to give out our room number left me speechless with fury.

I stuffed the note into my pocket and tried Bryana's phone but it was switched off. Frustrated, I left a voice message that I was on my way to collect her and, no arguments, she must wait until I got there. It would take me no more than fifteen minutes, quicker if I jogged. I made it in a little over ten and sent a text to announce my arrival while I got my breath back. Then I asked at reception for directions to the room where Célestin Reynaud was holding her meeting – at this hotel I had to plead a family emergency to get them to divulge the information.

Thankfully the meeting was still in progress. I eased the door open a crack, just enough to satisfy myself that Bryana was there and safe, then I parked my butt on a sofa right outside to wait.

"What are you doing here?" Bryana displayed her anger with venomous glare. "You don't need to check up on me."

"I'm not checking up on you." I kissed her on unresponsive lips and tried to hug her but she resisted me. "I just missed you, and wanted us to spend a little time together."

Clearly unconvinced, Bryana's body language repelled further intimacy although she did introduce me to Célestin.

"Enchanté." Célestin kissed me on both cheeks before she stepped back to give my body keen scrutiny. Célestin's tongue snaked across her lips as she turned back to Bryana. "Chérie, pourquoi n'avez-vous pas me dire votre nouvel ami était si sexy?"

A delicate flush infused Bryana's face. She flicked a very brief glance at me then turned back to Célestin. "Vraiment! Je n'avais pas remarqué."

I intervened to stop the exchange becoming embarrassing. "Now you've hurt my feelings, Bryana, I thought you might have noticed what was right under your nose." My exaggerated huff drew a glare from Bryana and a laugh from Célestin.

"Bryana, take this gorgeous woman away before I forget my manners and hit on her myself." Célestin's heavily accented English added a certain je ne sais quoi to the remark.

"You wouldn't dare." Bryana fired back a challenge, her eyes sparkling like highly polished sapphires.

"Try me, chérie."

"Come on." I reached for Bryana's arm but she batted my hand away.

"Leave me alone!" Her angry hiss was loud enough to reach my ears but not be audible to those around us.

I ignored her rejection and tried again. "How about a stroll and a quiet drink before we go back to the hotel?"

"Perfect!" Célestin leaned in to kiss Bryana on both cheeks before she turned to me and repeated the process, taking the opportunity to whisper, "Make her rest a little before we start work tomorrow."

"I'll try," I replied, smiling at the idea of making Bryana do anything she didn't want to do.

We left the hotel in silence and had walked several hundred yards before Bryana relaxed her stiff body. "What were you whispering about with Célestin?"

"Nothing important." I took Bryana's arm to steer her around a crowd of revelers spilling out from a bar onto the narrow street leading away from the canal. "Célestin cares about you, as I do. We both want to protect you and keep you safe."

"I don't need your protection." Bryana tried to pull away and stumbled, her high heels precarious on the uneven pavers.

I tightened my grip to stop her from falling.

Yes you do, my sweet, you just don't know how much.

The note was burning a hole on my pocket. Anger welled up, and my throat tightened but I managed to grind out a response. "You are fooling yourself if you think you're invincible."

Bryana huffed. "I can take care of myself."

"Like you did at Out of Bounds?"

Bryana stiffened visibly. "You sure know how to hit below the belt."

Concern for her safety had forced the accusation from my mouth before my brain engaged. I knew full well bringing up the trauma that was so fresh in her mind wasn't the way to win her over.

If I wanted Bryana to take me seriously I was going to have to tell her about the note but not here in the street. The bar I had earmarked earlier came into view. I ignored the outside tables as too public and guided her into the dimly lit interior.

Soft music mingled with voices in a variety of different languages as we threaded our way between the occupied tables toward the rear where several vacant booths offered both comfortable seating and an element of privacy. I ordered champagne, it was expensive but who cared? Cost was irrelevant when I needed to make a good impression, let's face it, the way things were right now any impression would be a start. A tense silence hung in the air between us. Gone was the relaxed mood that prevailed in the aftermath of our lovemaking this afternoon. Bryana fiddled with a coaster, twisting it between her fingers, looking anywhere but at me. While I cursed my loose tongue, assuming that she was still brooding over my unfortunate remark about Out of Bounds. What a fool I was to spoil things.

The arrival of the Taittinger Nocturne along with a dish of nibbles proved a welcome distraction from my thoughts. The server opened the champagne with deft movements and poured two glasses then left us the bottle in a wine chiller.

"Have you brought me here for a purpose?" Bryana regarded me suspiciously over the rim of her glass.

"Not really." I evaded the question, wanting to bide my time until a right moment presented itself – if there ever was a right moment to spring something like the note onto her. The tension had eased slightly with the advent of the wine, making me loath to introduce another inflammatory topic. "I just thought we deserved a little quiet time to wind down the busy day. How was your dinner?"

"Nice… Different." Bryana seemed happy to talk trivialities. "First we had a tray of mixed canapé, all sorts of delicious little savories, beautifully presented on a bed of banana leaves, followed by a tagine of lamb with a couscous salad and lemon mousse. How about you? Did you eat?" She sipped her wine appearing at ease.

"Steak and a large chocolate dessert."

"That figures." Bryana gave me a quizzical glance. "How you keep your figure I'll never know."

"Mostly with hard work." I grinned. "Keeping the estate running smoothly, and exercising the horses. Remember Tavish?"

"Only too well." Bryana shuddered and pulled a face. "Not one of my favorite memories."

"Tavish would be hurt to hear you say that." I shook my head in dismay. "He really enjoyed the experience. Although, he suggested that next time you might wear something more suitable."

"There isn't going to be a next time, not in this life."

"Oh dear, that's such a shame." I couldn't resist baiting her some more. "Especially after I sort of promised Tavish you'd come by and ride him again."

"In your dreams."

That's my problem in a nutshell. I can't stop dreaming about what we could have if Bryana... No, I mustn't go there yet. Enough that we have today, tonight, I can't look any further until we lay to rest the ghosts of the past.

"I'll tell him that you can't wait to come and see him."

"You'd do that to the poor animal?" Bryana grinned, playing along with my teasing.

"No." I reassured her. "Tavish is very special to me. I wouldn't want to hurt his feelings like that."

"Good." Bryana picked up a handful of rice crackers and nibbled on them.

Now she had relaxed a little more this seemed the ideal moment to raise the subject of the note. I hated to risk changing the mood or creating more problems for our fragile relationship but I had to warn Bryana. I couldn't take the chance of Esmée carrying out her threat and maybe doing something really dangerous, something neither of us were prepared for or could anticipate.

I took a deep breath. "Um… After dinner I went back to the hotel and found this pushed under our door." I fished the sheet of paper out of my pocket and passed it across the table.

"What?" Bryana unfolded the note, and scanned the writing for far longer than it would have taken her to read a couple of hundred lines before she raised her head her gaze troubled. "How did she know?"

I didn't need to ask who *she* was. "I imagine she guessed, or put two and two together based on your previous visits here."

"Yes, I suppose so. I am rather predictable." Bryana sighed. "Esmée would have known exactly where to find me. No wonder you made such a fuss about meeting me and you didn't say a word even when I gave you a hard time."

"There wasn't any point in making things a whole lot worse than they already were. You needed to come to terms with me hanging around like a guard dog."

Bryana nodded. "You have a point. I'll have to think about changing my routine in the future. From now, on wherever I go, I'll choose a different hotel to the one I've always favored and maybe even vary the airline I use to travel as well."

"Or you could let me take care of you… permanently." Again the words escaped my mouth before my thought process came to the rescue.

Shit! It was too soon to ask Bryana for that sort of commitment.

Even though in my own mind I was certain of my feelings, there were a number of stumbling blocks to overcome before...

"What are you saying?" Bryana gave me an incredulous look. "Are you asking me to...? No…" She shook her head.

I couldn't help but laugh at the look of horror on her face. "It's not such a bad idea. Think about it. We are good together in so many ways."

"No!"

"Why not?" To give myself something to do I topped up our glasses with the remaining champagne. My hand shook. The enormity of losing Bryana stared me in the face.

"Because…" Bryana ground to a halt and stared into her wine like it was the center of her universe.

"Bryana, honey, look at me." I waited while her head slowly lifted and her gaze met mine. "Do you trust me?"

She frowned. "I suppose I do…"

It was a heart stopping moment. She didn't sound very sure. I rested my hand on hers.

"Oh, honey," I held her gaze. "I know you're scared, but you have no reason to fear me. I won't let you down, ever, and we have a lot of talking still to do before anything else happens."

Bryana's lips parted, and her eyes widened questioningly, but she didn't speak. Maybe she didn't know what to say, or how to frame the questions uppermost in her mind. If that was the case I would need to fill in the blanks and help her make some sense of the situation.

"This isn't a five minute fix, we have a long way to go, we'd hardly scratched the surface before Esmée stepped in and ruined everything. Right now our main priority must be to rebuild what we already had, only then can we begin to move forward one step at a time.

Please be assured, I will never ask for more than you can or want to give. We can move at your pace and stop any time you feel uncomfortable."

"You make it sound so easy..."

Optimist that I am, I read the shake of Bryana's head as uncertainty rather that outright rejection. "It will be." My tone was deliberately positive to counter any negativity on her part. "I know you'll come up with all sorts of arguments against a permanent relationship, like your career and our places of residence but these are things that can be overcome with a little thought. You have to remember Scotland isn't at the end of the world, London is only a couple of hours away by air." I didn't dare let on that getting to the airport was a marathon that often took far longer than the flight itself. "You can also fly direct to just about anywhere in the world from Scotland. Also, I'm totally flexible these days, I can't see any obstacle that would prevent us from dividing our time between the two places as your job dictates."

Bryana took a sip of champagne before responding. "You really think we stand a chance of making this work?"

"Yes." I nodded emphatically. "We have nothing to lose by trying. And, with me around to keep an eye on you, Esmée and Marisa had better watch their step."

"That sounds good to me." Bryana smiled. "I would hate to get on the wrong side of you. You scared the hell out of me, a few times, in the beginning."

"I scared you?" Shit! No wonder Bryana had wanted to keep me at arm's length. I couldn't believe she hadn't said something before. "When? How?"

"When you turned up on my doorstep throwing your weight around as if you owned me. Then later... later you made me feel like a slut, a whore, who deserved no better than to be used.

"I am so sorry, honey." This was a terrible indictment. "I never meant for you to feel that way. Misconceptions on both sides led to a few issues, for sure, but we've got those sorted now. We can start over, as of tonight. No baggage. No past. A clean slate. Do you agree?"

"Yes." Bryana reached for my hand. "Then tomorrow you can ride shotgun while I work."

"Done!" I raised her fingers to my lips to seal the bargain. "Damn! I want to kiss you properly. Shall we go back to the hotel?"

"Yes, please, I'd like that."

Full Circle

Bryana

*Can Cassie keep Bryana safe and provide
the discipline she needs?*

The decorated façade of Amsterdam's Rijks Museum provided a perfect backdrop for Célestin Reynaud's collection of day wear. The wide concourse offered ample space for the models to parade in groups, and singly, or occasionally stop to strike a pose in one of the three arches that formed the imposing entrance. Célestin had been lucky to get permission to use an area that would normally be thronged with tourists at this time of the day, but with the main museum closed for renovations visitors were directed to a different entrance around the corner in the annex.

"That's very good, Alexis." I nodded encouragement to the final model in the set. "Just a shade more of that sexy hip movement, please. Perfect!" The motorized shutter whirred almost continuously as I fired off dozens of shots in rapid succession, moving around as I did so to capture the elegant suit from as many different angles as possible. "Okay that'll do for now, Alexis. Thanks everyone. Just the final group shots then we're done." The models dispersed quickly, rushing toward the converted RV that served as a mobile dressing room when Célestin was on location for a quick check on hair and makeup.

There was a round of applause from the watching crowd. While changing cameras I took the opportunity to glance behind me. A number of people had gathered behind a taped cordon to watch the fashion shoot but I was only interested in one person.

My gaze homed in on Cassie Stuart. My lover, the woman who kept me sane, satisfied, and safe. Unmistakable in her usual attire of a plaid shirt worn over a white vest, jeans, and ankle boots. Too damned sexy for words. Heat sizzled through my body. She'd had an effect on me from day one. However, it'd taken me quite a while and much soul searching to accept that Cassie had held my heart hostage ever since she rescued me from a cold, wet, and very miserable night on a bleak Scottish mountain. The events of the past few days, since our arrival in Amsterdam, had finally confirmed her place in my life. Although it had been touch and go for a while as circumstances tested our relationship to breaking point.

Cassie leaned casually against a tree a few yards away from the main group of spectators. She appeared outwardly relaxed and disinterested in anything other than the fashion show, but I knew that was a front. Behind those dark glasses her eyes would be busily scanning the crowd for danger. In particular for a glimpse of Esmée Vincent, my ex, who still posed a considerable threat to me eight months after the end of our turbulent relationship. Esmée was here, in Amsterdam – at least I assumed she was. Somebody had delivered the note containing her latest threat to my hotel room on Monday night. Although Marisa, her lover, had a role in the catalog shoot I doubted she was responsible. Esmée's insidious presence dominated our lives and impinged on everything we did. It was now Thursday, the last day of the shoot, and Esmée's continued absence from the scene was giving me the jitters. Not that I wanted any contact with her, but the lack of some tangible sighting was singularly unnerving.

With one final, lingering glance at Cassie I picked up the two cameras I planned to use for this session hung one around my neck and turned back to work. Impatient to begin, I fired off a few shots as the models emerged spasmodically from the RV and assembled according to the plan set out for the finale. Another hour at the most and I'd be free to spend some quality time with my love.

Cassie had promised me a special treat to celebrate the rebirth of our relationship. After several false starts we both hoped this new beginning would mature naturally into the permanence we both desired. In this instance I had no idea what she meant by special since I considered all the time we spent together special. Clearly though, Cassie had her own ideas and as she was being somewhat secretive about the arrangements, I would have to wait until later to find out what they were.

Meanwhile, I concentrated on getting the best from the disparate group of models. "Wonderful, ladies." With a sweep of my hand I directed them to move and reform, as per the rehearsal plan. To my amazement the choreography worked. The group flowed en masse, creating a seamlessly evolving pattern like a flock of birds in the sky. I followed every movement with the cameras, sometimes closing in and other times drawing back.

Finally this part was done. The next stage, the selection of the best shots for the catalog would take time and close study by myself in conjunction with the production team.

"Perfect!" Célestin stepped out of the RV to congratulate the whole team. "Thank you all for working so hard this week."

There was a burst of applause followed by a mass exodus. The models rushed to change into street clothes before they drifted away alone or in groups, then hair and make-up left, too. Wardrobe always took much longer to pack up as did I.

Célestin appeared at my side when I had almost finished fitting my cameras into their traveling bag. "A word, Bryana." She linked arms with me, then led me out of the RV and a short distance away from any listeners before she spoke.

"You and Cassie have sorted out your differences?" Very neatly she'd turned the statement into a question.

"Yes, I think we have..." I flicked a glance to where my lover waited. "How did you know?"

"Simple logic, chérie..." Célestin shook her head, and a smile formed on her lips. "I saw how troubled you were on Monday and now... Now you're a totally different woman. Sex is a wonderful healer."

Heat swept across my face. "Is it that obvious?"

"It is to me." Célestin kissed me warmly. "I am so pleased for you. You deserve some happiness after the way that bitch Esmée treated you."

"You knew?"

"Everybody did, chérie."

"Oh!" Her revelation robbed me of speech. Had I born the scars for all to see? That thought appalled me.

"That woman is cruel, and manipulative. In my opinion, you are well out of it. Marisa is now the favored one... She and Esmée are two of a kind they deserve each other, but I doubt it will last. Quite frankly, I would prefer not to use Marisa, she is a disruptive influence, but she is the perfect shape for my designs." Célestin gave a Gallic shrug. "Good models are like gold dust and business is business."

"Working with Marisa doesn't bother me," I said, hastening to reassure her. Not strictly true, but I didn't want to create problems for Célestin. This week had been particularly difficult with the threat hanging over me and Marisa being obstructive at every turn. Nothing big or too obvious, however, just niggly little things. Marisa, like all models, knew how not to step over the line; getting a bad reputation would see her losing out on the more lucrative bookings.

"That's very generous of you, chérie." Célestin hugged me. "I must let you go, Cassie has been very patient but…" She waved to Cassie who pushed away from the tree and sauntered over to us.

"Hello, chérie." Célestin greeted Cassie warmly, kissing her on both her cheeks. "Take Bryana away, now, she needs a break from work and some serious TLC."

"I have that all in hand." Cassie winked. She turned to me, her eyes sparkling with amusement. "Are you ready now, honey?"

"Almost. I just need to collect my stuff and then we can go."

"Get a move on then." Cassie gave me a playful tap on the ass as I turned to leave.

Wearing a smile on my face I walked toward the RV to collect my camera case. Then I came face to face with Marisa lurking in the doorway and the smile faded.

Has she been waiting all this time just to confront me?

"Out of my way, bitch!" Her dark eyes flashed menacingly. "Don't get too cozy with Cassie Stuart, your time together is about to come to an end. Nobody gets away with crossing Esmée. She has your card marked."

Marisa brushed me roughly aside and was gone before I could draw breath let alone utter a word. What could I have said anyway? I had no idea what any of her cryptic comments meant. They sounded like threats but... I shook my head. How could either she or Esmée influence my relationship with Cassie?

With Marisa's snarky comments still buzzing in my head, I picked up the camera bag then reached into the locker for my purse and came out empty handed. I frowned. Shit! Why wasn't it where I'd left it? After a frantic search I found the purse on the floor in the shoe sized space underneath the lockers. I quickly checked the contents were intact then went back out to join Cassie and Célestin who, in my absence, had become involved in a serious discussion. It took me a few seconds to tune into the subject and a couple more to check I was hearing it right. Amazing! I'd never have guessed that Célestin was into bondage, particularly rope play. Yet Cassie had drawn it out of her in a few short minutes.

"You must come to Scotland, to Auchtercairn." Cassie acknowledged my return with a quirk of her brow then she slipped one hand casually across my shoulder and drew me close. "Bryana will confirm I run a well equipped dungeon. With something to suit every kink be it extreme pain, exquisite pleasure, or some place in between."

"Indeed she does." I grinned. "It's like walking into a fantasy world. I could hardly believe my eyes when I stumbled on the dungeon and found all manner of equipment just waiting to be used. I have to say though, I found the stone-walled tower a bit foreboding at first but it soon grows on you and it's a perfect setting for the instruments of torture and pleasure within."

"A tower?" Célestin's eyes widened.

"Oh! Didn't I say?" Cassie suddenly looked very pleased with herself. "Auchtercairn is a seventeenth century castle. The real deal. Come and see for yourself. We can have a serious session with the ropes or anything else you'd like to try." She fished a business card out of her pocket and handed it to Célestin. "Call me and we'll fix a date that suits us all. I have a film crew there at the moment, shooting something dark and horrific, but they'll be gone in a little over six weeks."

Célestin smiled, her gaze swept Cassie's body from head to toe and back again in the blink of an eye. "Yes, I will, I would like that, very much. Maybe later, sometime in October."

I feared Célestin's interest in Cassie went much deeper than a session in the dungeon. Confirmation came with a brief flick of her tongue across slightly parted lips – a perfect imitation of a cat with a bowl of cream. I hoped Cassie knew what she was getting into. Célestin could be a predator when it came to satisfying her sexual desires.

Somewhere close by the musical chimes of a clock heralded the hour, Célestin pulled a face and glanced around at the RV. "I must go. Our permit is about to expire and I don't want to upset the authorities." She kissed us both and hurried away.

Cassie turned me to face her. "Want to tell me what happened back there?" She indicated the RV with a nod.

"Search me." I shrugged, attempting to keep my tone casual so as not to worry her. "Just Marisa being bitchy. What she said didn't make any sense."

"Mmmm, I knew I should have gone with you." Cassie dropped a light kiss on my forehead. "Put her out of your mind. We have better things to do than dwell on that sneaky cow." She picked up my camera bag and took my hand. Despite my outwardly relaxed mood, the leisurely stroll back to the hotel wasn't the pleasant experience it should have been. I couldn't get the brush with Marisa out of my mind.

What did she mean about Cassie?

How has Esmée marked my card and for what purpose?

I couldn't fathom out what was going on with those two, or why Esmée was targeting me.

Later, I took my time in the shower mulling over the day's events and the pleasures still to come. Cassie waylaid me as I emerged from the bathroom her mind clearly focused on pleasures of another kind. I tried really hard to respond to her overtures, but I couldn't melt into her arms and her gentle kisses failed to ignite the fire like she usually did.

"What's up, honey?" Cassie stroked gentle fingers down my neck and across my shoulders. "You are so tense. Why don't I give you a relaxing massage before we go out to dinner?"

My first instinct was to decline, as I always did when she raised the subject. I could never see the point. Then I thought why not?

What have I got to lose?

Cassie was always harping on about her famous massage skills, maybe it was time I gave her relaxation technique a try. I certainly needed something to soothe away my stress and dispel the turmoil that Marisa had stirred up.

My tentative nod of agreement produced a swift reaction from Cassie. Before I could blink or change my mind she'd dispensed with the towel I wore and spread it out on my bed, then she added a couple more for good measure. Cassie obviously meant business this afternoon.

"Make yourself comfortable. I won't be a minute." Cassie disappeared into the bathroom.

In her absence I arranged myself on the bed face down, with my eyes closed, and arms loosely by my sides. Cassie returned to the room and I heard her moving about but in an effort to distance myself from events I didn't open my eyes. A few moments later she approached the bed. "Are you ready, honey?"

Am I?

Yeah! No point in delaying the inevitable.

"As ready as I'll ever be." My jocular confirmation was a thinly disguised attempt to hide my deep seated distrust of alternative therapies. Skeptic that I am, I wasn't entirely convinced by Cassie's faith in massage. Could it really be the magical cure-all she claimed? Seemed like I was about to find out.

"Take some deep breaths and empty your mind of clutter." Cassie's tone was calm, neutral and very professional.

Before I had time to do what she asked, a warm liquid trickled across my shoulders and over my back. A strange perfume reached my senses – intense, spicy, and sweet, like walking through a glade of tropical flowers – very hypnotic, yet not as totally overpowering as one might imagine. Her fingers traced the same path gliding across my neck and shoulders, then moved slowly down my spine.

"Just relax. You are still too tense," Cassie scolded, when my body reacted to her touch by tensing up.

Her oil slick fingers returned to my neck kneading the muscles gently before they swept out across my shoulders and then down my flank only to go back and repeat the circuit. With each long sweep along my rib cage, her fingers just brushed the edge of my tits. The action sent pulses of sensation rushing headlong through me.

My body suddenly began to hum to a sexual tune.

If nothing else, I'll get smooth skin and a sexual lift from the massage.

I sucked in a long breath.

"Good."

I thought I detected a hint of laughter in Cassie's voice.

Her hands slid slowly down until her fingers spanned my waist and her thumbs rested either side of my spine. "Now take another deep a breath and relax some more." She tightened her grip slightly to put a little pressure on my waist as if squeezing the tension out of me. "Forget the past, it's gone and you can't do anything to change it. Let all those bad memories drift away. Imagine them floating into space then being sucked into an enormous black hole never to be seen again."

Her fingers relaxed and moved lower, to massage the cheeks of my butt, her thumbs sliding into the crack and around the base. The breath caught in my throat when she came close to my slit but she never quite touched anything sensitive. Cassie moved on, her oil slick hands gliding over my skin, following the shape of my thighs, calves, and ankles until she reached my feet.

I turned over on her command and half opened my eyes to discover Cassie was naked, too. I hadn't actually thought about her need for clothes but I suppose it made sense. Better than spoiling good clothes with massage oil.

I'd never realized before how erotic a foot massage could be. Cassie worked on every part, manipulating my toes, stroking my insteps, and the soles of my feet – Lucky I'm not ultra sensitive in that area.

Are feet erogenous zones?

"Take deep even breaths," she intoned softly, working on my toes like she was milking the tension out of me. "Force all that negative energy from your body. You are in control of your own life. Concentrate on the positive aspects and the path you will take to move forward into the future."

Cassie slowly moved back up my legs. Her face a mask of concentration. At which point she climbed onto the bed and knelt over me, straddling my legs. From that position she continued the massage, again straying only briefly into the sensitive area between my thighs. My anticipation gathered pace. Certain that she was about to touch me intimately, my body reacted with a rush of moisture to the throbbing heart of my sex. However, she carried on upward until she reached my breasts.

Oh, the exquisite pleasure of being touched, the sensual delight in the lightness of her fingers on my skin. I wanted more, more, more.

She leaned forward to run her fingers over my shoulders and our bodies met flesh on flesh. A spark of raw energy drew a gasp from my lips but her concentration didn't waiver. It was as if she was in a trance, or inhabiting a different world to mine – somewhere detached from reality where nothing overtly sexual was happening, at least not for her. I, on the other hand, was totally fired up, with my body on the verge of total meltdown.

Cassie paused to drizzle a little more oil from a small bottle onto my chest. This brief respite from the sexual tension barely gave me time to catch my breath before, inevitably, Cassie took off again. Her fingers spread the film across my skin, gliding lazily through the fragrant oil, massaging my throat, moving over my breasts, and circling my nipples. I could hardly keep from crying out, from begging her to grant me the relief I so badly needed, but her air of detachment held me back.

Finally, Cassie put me out of my misery. She sat back on her heels and ran her hands down my body one last time. This time her oil-slick fingers gravitated to my throbbing center. With delicate movements she parted my labia and made contact with my clit.

An intense physical shockwave raced through my body. I bucked wildly, and tried to spread my legs but her knees either side of my thighs stopped me moving far.

"Keep still," Cassie said, suddenly emerging from her trance-like state. "Let me finish what I started."

Sex in a straightjacket. The frustration of being trapped almost drove me insane. Yet, on another level, being constrained was incredibly erotic. Cassie kept her movements to the bare minimum. The softest touch, the briefest tweak of my clit and then her oil-slick fingers slipped gently into my hole. No need for lubrication, I was plenty wet enough. She pushed deep, and the action sent her thumb skidding across my clit. I couldn't hold back. My muscles contracted drawing her deeper into me as my orgasm exploded.

"Oh, fuck! Fuck me! Please..." From a distance I heard a disassociated voice screaming profanities and begging for more. Not until I began to slide down from the peak did the voice register as my own.

A wave of surprise and embarrassment swept over me.

Did I really let go like that?

Cassie slumped forward, her body atop mine, her breathing fast yet fairly shallow. I could feel her heart racing, matching my own beat for beat. Had she come? I'd been so caught up in my own climactic event to register her actions or reactions.

Her lips found mine in a long, deep, lingering kiss that evolved into a mutual expression of sensual pleasure. Bare flesh smoothed against bare flesh, limbs intertwined, and fingers stroked those hard to reach places, raising the sexual tension to mind blowing heights. I couldn't believe I was ready to come again so soon. Cassie did things to my libido that no other woman had ever achieved.

My orgasm, when it came, was muted but powerful enough to rock my world. Almost simultaneously, Cassie ground her lower body hard against mine, her limbs trembling as her own climax raged apace.

A feeling of total contentment washed over me. Even had I not been pinned to the bed by Cassie's weight resting on me, I couldn't have moved a muscle. Enveloped in post sex lethargy I dozed, we probably both did, until Cassie shook me gently awake.

"Time to move, honey."

I stretched, and groaned, my body protesting with the effects of our recent sexual exploits.

Do I have to?

"Come on, honey." Cassie snickered. As if she read the unspoken question in my eyes. "After all that exercise I'm hungry for my dinner."

We showered together. The act of washing each other adding to and extending the pleasure of our new found intimacy. The need to give rather than take overwhelmed me. I dropped to my knees and worshiped Cassie with my tongue. Water cascaded over my back. She widened her stance to give me better access. Then she placed her hands on the back of my head and pushed my face into her sex. I lapped and sucked until she bucked against me, shouting my name as she climaxed; squirting a burst of hot cum onto my tongue.

Cassie pulled me to my feet and pushed me back against the tiled wall trapping me with her solid body. Then she bent her head and kissed me hard, forcing my lips apart and swirling her tongue around my mouth.

Suddenly Cassie pulled back from the kiss, and released me. "Get yourself dressed," she said, slapping me playfully across the ass as I moved toward the bedroom in search of a towel.

I'd learned a lot from the fashion industry over the years, not least the art of making a quick change. From a standing start, like today, I could achieve the full transformation in a little over fifteen minutes.

Cassie hadn't said where she was taking me to dinner so it was a pleasant surprise to discover that Cassie, a confirmed carnivore, had taken account of my tastes and booked us into a restaurant that specialized in seafood with not a single item of red meat on the menu. Our table on the outside terrace was perfect. Subdued lighting with candles in beautiful fluted glass shades that protected the flame from a breeze, a stunning view over a small water garden and soft music all added to the romantic ambience.

We shared a small mixed seafood platter. Oysters, scallops, crab legs, lobster, and baby squid sat alongside succulent shrimps, slivers of raw tuna, and fingers of salmon all garnished with wedges of lemon. Bowls of mayonnaise and an oriental dipping sauce completed the dish. I say shared, but all Cassie actually did was pick at the lobster and the shrimps, leaving most of the rest to me.

While we waited on the main course I brought up something that was puzzling me. "How did you and

Célestin get onto the subject of bondage? I'd never have known she was into anything like that if you hadn't drawn it out of her."

Cassie smiled. "She was easy to read. I dropped a subtle hint and she hooked onto it instantly. The look in her eyes gave the game away."

"Fair enough..." I sighed, now more confused by what she hadn't said. What line of subtly got the sort of reaction she wanted? "The bit I don't get is what prompted you to drop a hint in the first place or do you do it with everybody you meet?"

"Not everybody, no, but more often than not I slip a little something into the conversation just out of curiosity." Her lips twitched with the makings of a smile. "You'd be surprised how many people take the bait."

"Really?" I shook my head in amazement. I couldn't believe she had the nerve to bring up the subject with a total stranger but that was what set Cassie and myself apart. She oozed confidence. Her commanding presence meant people didn't question her authority or her right to pose probing questions. I'd die of embarrassment before broaching half the subjects she did.

"Yes, really." Cassie put heavy emphasis on her response, although the tables were far enough apart to allow for private conversation, she had dropped her voice to a loud whisper. "Of course, not everyone who responds is into the serious stuff. Most people are a little turned on by the idea of being tied up. There is a lot of fiction about right now that plays to the mindset of the furry handcuffs brigade but as you already know that sort of titillation bears no relationship to the lifestyle. There's a big difference between people who are looking to spice up their boring sex lives with what they see as naughty kink and people like us who get the whole lifestyle angle.

"I'm not sure I do get *it* anymore." I expelled a sigh. "I thought I did. Sasha talked me through the basics before Esmée came along and trashed everything. You have helped me to understand the difference between abuse and freedom of choice. Unfortunately though, your help has simply revealed gaping holes in what I thought I knew...both about myself and about being a submissive."

"You're doing great, honey." Cassie covered my hand with hers. Her index finger moving in small circles on my wrist calmed my rising agitation. "It'll all fall into place again given time. We can work on the detail bit by bit until you feel comfortable with everything. This isn't a race against the clock, we can take as long as necessary. The main thing to remember is that I want you to find the experience stimulating both emotionally and physically. And for it to make a real difference to your life.

"That sounds good to me."

The conversation was halted by the arrival of our main course. Cassie had followed my lead in choosing a fillet of salmon cooked *en papillote* with ginger, chilli, scallion, honey, and soy. The fish was served with rice and a selection of steamed baby vegetables.

Cassie lifted the first forkful of fish to her mouth cautiously, frowning slightly as if unsure of the taste, then she nodded. "Mmm, This is really good. I can see now why you like fish so much."

"It's more that I'm not keen on red meat – steak in particular." I took a sip of the excellent Riesling Cassie had selected to go with our meal. "I do eat meat occasionally, and poultry too."

Cassie nodded, as if she understood where I was coming from. "With me it's ingrown, until now, a total rejection of anything with scales and fins. I had a bad experience with fish when I was young and it's stuck with me ever since." She took another bite. "However, this is absolutely delicious. I can see you'll have to educate my palate and I'll do the same with you. Have you tried venison?"

"No." I shuddered. "Poor Bambi."

Cassie's loud snort drew immediate attention from the other diners. She shook her head and lowered her voice. "That's a very shortsighted reaction. The production of venison for the table has nothing to do with cute little fawns being preyed upon by evil hunters with guns. Responsible landowners cull the wild deer to keep the numbers balanced, so there is enough natural food to see the remainder through the harsh winter months."

"I'd never thought about it in those terms before." I was somewhat taken aback by her vehement response.

"It's a simple enough equation: too many deer per acre means none of them have enough to eat and then a lot more perish both from the cold and starvation. Besides which, nowadays most of the venison produced for the table is from farmed deer, just like sheep and cattle. Farming makes perfect sense if you want to ensure the quality of the end product."

"Oh, I never realized you could farm deer."

"Indeed you can." Cassie topped up our wine glasses. "Hark at me, I didn't bring you out for a romantic meal to lecture you."

"You weren't lecturing," I quickly reassured her. "My reaction was based on false sentimentality. Besides, I'm all in favor of sustainability. Many types of fish are farmed for that reason."

"See, that proves my point, there really isn't any difference when you think about it." She grinned and returned to her meal.

I put my fork down on an empty plate a few seconds before Cassie did the same.

"That was really good." Cassie folded her napkin neatly and placed it on the table "The flavors blended so well and I liked the way they presented the vegetables."

"Me too." I smiled. "I must recreate that dish at home. Are you game to try my version?"

Cassie nodded. "Only if I can tempt you into trying something too. I'm thinking I might use those ingredients as a marinade with venison steak. Although I'd probably swap the soy for whisky to complement the cranachan I'd serve for dessert."

"Cran-a-kan?" I stumbled over the unfamiliar word.

"Near enough." Cassie laughed. "A traditional Scottish dessert containing raspberries, cream, honey, whisky and toasted oatmeal."

"You're on. How can I possibly refuse such a tempting menu?"

Cassie frowned like she wasn't sure if I was being facetious. "Anyway..." She fixed me with a penetrating gaze. "Tell me a bit more about Célestin. How long have you known her? What's her history?"

"A little over ten years. She has a lot of experience in the haute couture field. Latterly, she worked for Hervé as his première vendeuse before setting up her own label just over three years ago."

"Does she have a partner?"

I shook my head. "Not currently, at least as far as I'm aware she doesn't, I'm not that close to her socially. There have been a couple of relationships in the past but none of them lasted more than a few months. Célestin is a sexual butterfly. She likes variety – one nighter's, and the sort of ephemeral passionate affairs one finds in a constantly fluctuating society. With several big fashion shows each year, plus quite a few smaller events, she gets to travel a lot and to take her pick from a wide selection of the available talent.

"Interesting... Have you and she ever...?" Cassie quirked her brow interrogatively.

"No, we haven't." I snickered, finding the idea of Célestin and me having a sexual fling amusing to say the least. We were oil and water when it came to sexual attraction. "I don't register anywhere on her gaydar meter or her on mine. Célestin has a predilection for the more androgynous models and also for butch types, like you, so you'd better watch your step. I imagine you're ringing the ten bell with her... As you did with me."

Crap!

I regretted that last bit the second it left my lips. The admission was a little too revealing.

"Ten eh? Thank you, honey, that is very gratifying." A dark flush swept across Cassie's face and then faded in an instant. "Perhaps I should mention here that while Célestin is welcome to visit the dungeon for some serious play, I'm not available to her on a sexual level." Cassie winked. "That place my bed is taken, permanently."

"Oh, yes, I see..." Heat suffused my face. This was the first time Cassie had made a clear distinction between what happened in the dungeon and in real life. It brought home to me how little I actually knew about her life and what made her tick. With everything else going on, since our reunion, we'd hardly had time to dot all the i's and cross all the t's. It was one thing to talk about the dungeon as if it were a normal workplace but a totally different thing to face up to the reality of what went on. I didn't know how I would feel when the time came for Cassie to have a client or whatever she called the folks who came to use her services. However, tension churned in my stomach, if we were to have a successful relationship I would have to come to terms with that aspect of her life.

"Just an idea, honey... I know you and I still have some serious talking to do about that side of our relationship. How do you feel, in principle, about the three of us getting together in the dungeon sometime? Nothing heavy, a little light bondage to test the waters. It might help you to understand the difference between my public and private persona."

"I like Célestin a lot but..." The idea of a threesome with Célestin was a bit beyond my comfort zone. The intimacy of being naked and vulnerable didn't sit alongside the strictly business relationship we shared.

"That's fine, honey. I don't want to rush you into anything... I can do Célestin on her own if it makes you uncomfortable. Or, providing she agrees, you could maybe sit in and observe."

"I think I'd like that better."

"Okay, honey." She raised my hand to her lips and kissed the tips of my fingers. "One step at a time. Whatever makes you happy. Now how about we order some dessert?"

Cassie studied the dessert menu intently before she selected two fancy chocolate confections without consulting me first. My raised eyebrow caught her eye and she grinned sheepishly. "I'm celebrating. Okay! These are both for me. I know you don't care for rich desserts. How about I order you a plate of fruit?"

"Yes, please. Fruit would be good."

Later, we sauntered back to the hotel along the narrow streets. Cassie kept me close, with her arm around my waist, as we mingled with the crowds of tourists most of them gawping at the scantily clad girls who posed in lighted windows.

We turned into another street, leaving the crowds behind as we headed for the hotel. The darkness gave me confidence to raise a new topic. "I think I'd like to know a bit more about rope play."

Cassie's stride faltered fractionally. "What brought that on, honey?"

"This business with Célestin, I suppose. You were both so enthused in your discussion on rope play, it caught my interest although the topic has been on my mind for quite a while. After what happened in the club I was a mess, but something about the way those bitches tied me up struck a chord in my mind..."

"Go on," Cassie prompted.

I hesitated, waiting until we'd entered the hotel and crossed the lobby to the elevator before I continued.

"I just thought you might explain some of the simple but effective ways to use ropes in play. I've not had any experience in that field. Sasha always uses handcuffs, Esmée did too, apart from that one time when she and Marisa kidnapped me and what those two did to me that night could never be described as play..." A shiver trickled down my spine and I drew a shaky breath into my lungs.

Will I ever get the memory of what happened at Out of Bounds into perspective?

"I can show you. A hands on demonstration is much better than me just explaining," Cassie said, ushering me into our room and double locking the door. "We can do it now if you want."

So soon!

"I hadn't actually thought about now." I took a step away from her.

"No time like the present." Cassie gave me a sideways glance. "You're not backing away from the idea already? I have some rope in my bag."

My throat tightened around the lump that suddenly formed there.

Cassie carries ropes with her?

I couldn't meet her gaze but sensed it was fixed firmly on me. My face heated and my heart hammered in my chest.

"Bryana, honey, are you all right?"

"What?" The concern in Cassie's voice pulled me back from the bad place. "Yes, I'm fine..." I attempted to portray a semblance of normality to give me time to recover my equilibrium. "Just a little surprised to find that you carried rope on this trip."

Where did she expect to use it and on whom?

"I never travel without my gear." Cassie hauled her bag out of the closet, unzipped a side pocket, and pulled out a couple of hanks of white silky cord. "One never knows when it will come in handy, like now." She slipped the clip off one hank to let the rope unwind slowly through her fingers and snake about our feet.

Her lips twitched; no doubt in amusement at my discomfort. I knew I was being stupid getting all worked up over a bit of rope. Worse still, since I'd been the one to raise the topic. Cassie was simply doing what came naturally to her. She wasn't showing off, play acting or living in a fantasy world. Her lifestyle choice was as important to her as eating and breathing. If I wanted to share her life – and I did – then I must shed my inhibitions, embrace her culture, and whatever the future held for us.

"Get undressed then sit on the bed." Cassie's businesslike tone brooked no argument.

I did as she said, although taking some time to hang my clothes in the closet, put my shoes away, and use the bathroom.

Still fully dressed, Cassie moved to stand alongside the bed, the rope now draped around her neck.

Cassie reached for my leg stroking her hand down the shin to my ankle. "Relax, honey," she said softly.

She seems to be having to say that to me a lot lately.

I chastised myself and made a conscious effort to control my reactions.

"There is nothing to be afraid of." She held a strand out toward me. "Here, touch it. Feel how soft it is.

I put my hand out and closed my fingers around the cord. It was indeed soft, and much smoother than I'd imagined it would be. My concern began to dissipate. I trusted Cassie; trusted she wasn't going to do anything to hurt me. Put simply, I had to conquer my deep seated fears of being tied up, of the tight bindings cutting into my flesh, of the excruciating pain, and the not knowing if escape or discovery was possible. That was the worst part of the memory.

I took several deep breaths and let go of the cord. "I think I'm ready now."

Cassie nodded her approval. "You're doing great, honey. Keep in mind what I'm doing now is just for demonstration. I won't normally tie you up like this but I want you see what is happening and to get an idea of what to expect."

"Okay."

Cassie ran the length of cord through her hands to roughly half way. "Just watch what I'm doing and you'll see this is very different to what happened to you in London. For a start, I'm not tying any complicated or hard to release knots." Then she wound that piece loosely around both my ankles, twisting it several times in the middle before she brought the remainder up to do the same to my wrists.

Being able to see what was happening and having Cassie talk me through the procedure made a tremendous difference, as did the fact that the cord wasn't tight.

"How does that feel?" Cassie tweaked the length of rope that spanned the distance between my wrists and ankles. "Move your feet about, don't be afraid, see how it affects your hands and vice versa."

"Oh...that's awfully strange." Laughter bubbled in my throat and emerged as a giggle. "I feel a bit like a puppet."

"That's really good, honey." Now I want to take this off and show you something else. "Watch how easily the rope comes undone."

I tried to follow how she did it but quickly lost track after she caught one end, pulled, twisted, and suddenly the whole lot came free.

Cassie tried a couple more configurations before declaring the first lesson over. "That was excellent, honey. I know how difficult this is for you, you're being really brave. We'll try some more examples once we get back to London." She re-coiled the rope, secured it with the clip, then put it away in her bag and took me to her bed.

We arrived back in London late on Friday giving me precious few days to reorganize my gear and relax before I was due to leave for my next assignment in New York at the end of the following week. I had no idea how Cassie would react to my imminent departure across the Atlantic. With so much happening in Amsterdam I hadn't got around to breaking the news of another trip to her. As things turned out I needn't have worried about her reaction.

"I'm not letting you go all that way on your own," Cassie said, making the decision to accompany me in an instant. She even insisted on paying the difference to upgrade my economy ticket to business class. – a luxury I rarely allowed myself.

"If you're sure." I grinned, then stepped in to hug her. "I'll have to get you accreditation, as my assistant, so you can come backstage, if you'd like to, that is."

"Will Célestin be in New York?"

"No, sorry, she won't." I stifled a pang of jealousy at her eagerness to renew Célestin's acquaintance. "This isn't the main New York fashion week – that is usually in February and September, just before London. This event is for young graduate designers to showcase their work." Would Cassie be disappointed that she couldn't hook up with Célestin?

"Not a problem." Cassie shrugged. "I just thought it might be rather nice for the three of us to get better acquainted. Maybe go out to eat together or something."

Her reaction relieved some of my concern. "We can do that next time." Damn! That wouldn't have made much sense to Cassie. She wasn't familiar with the fashion show calendar and would need some clarification. "Even if you don't make it to the fashion week in New York at the beginning of September, Célestin will be here, in London, the following week."

"Excellent, honey. Maybe afterwards we all can travel up to Auchtercairn together the film people should have gone by then."

"I'm afraid not." I shook my head. "After London the whole circus moves to Milan and then to Paris. We won't be through there until the beginning of October."

"Even better. The weather by then is usually perfect for walking and riding the horses." She threw me a challenging grin. "I know that Tavish will be very pleased to see you again. Then in the evenings the three of us can relax in the great hall or explore our compatibility in the dungeon."

"Sounds perfect...apart from the horse bit. I'm not that keen on riding." Understatement of the year. Make that, I never want to ride a horse again.

"Nonsense, honey." Cassie smirked. "I'd say you're a natural. Riding without a saddle or stirrups requires a special skill and balance. You did five miles without once coming off."

I shook my head. Little did she know how close I came to doing just that, but not in the way she'd meant.

Over the next few days Cassie demonstrated several more basic bondage techniques until I became totally comfortable with being tied up. I'd always known I needed some level of constraint but it came as a surprise to find how readily I took to rope play. Like a drug addict, my body craved just a little more each time.

She fed my craving bit by bit, carefully explaining in detail what she was doing, never taking too big a step forward and always leaving me wanting. Although we hadn't tried any bondage in anger so to speak I knew that would be the inevitable next step, the prospect of doing a proper scene was always on my mind. However, I doubted we would get around to anything more serious with the trip to New York imminent.

Cassie's packing consisted of throwing a few casual clothes into a bag and she was ready to go. Her needs were simple a couple of vests with toning shirts, a spare pair of jeans, and her underwear. Even with the practice of years it took me several hours and much fiddling to achieve a neatly packed bag that contained everything I needed for the trip.

The actual flight to New York passed off smoothly. After we'd battled a crowded terminal at Heathrow, and negotiated the lengthy queues at both check-in and security, we sought the peaceful oasis of the business lounge to sit out the usual interminable wait before boarding. Having Cassie for company plus the added luxury of seats in business class made a vast difference to the trip. At JFK we shunned the long queue for the shuttle bus in favor of the Air Train to Jamaica, followed by the subway right into Manhattan and my favorite hotel on West 40th Street. Expensive, but worth the extra money since it was convenient to all the places I visited on a regular basis without having to resort to the regular use of taxis or the subway.

"Does Esmée know you use this hotel?" Cassie quirked her brow as we waited our turn in the queue at reception.

"Yes, she does," I conceded. "She's stayed here with me more than once in the past. I always use this hotel when I'm in New York."

"I thought we'd settled this argument. Didn't we have a conversation on this very topic back in Amsterdam? Or did I just dream it?"

"No you didn't dream anything and yes, I did promise I was going to change my habits, but I'd already made this booking, plus the one in Berlin next week and then back here in September. Changing any of them at this late stage would be problematic or even nigh impossible. After we get home I promise I will take a long look at my schedule and make the necessary changes." I stepped forward to hand my passport and credit card to the receptionist before turning back to Cassie. "Anyway, I'm sure we're pretty safe from interference this week. Neither Esmée or Marisa have shown any interest in this event in the past."

Famous last words!

Having said that they were bound to turn up just to prove me a liar.

Cassie huffed. "That may well be the case, but I don't want you taking any chances. I will go everywhere with you just to be sure."

She kept her word, shadowing my every move during the five day visit. Once my photographic assignment finished, I had a couple of appointments with designers who were interested in using my services at future shows. I had sent them my resume and references but both wanted a face-to-face meeting before committing to a contract.

"Do you really need to drum up more business?" Cassie asked, as we left the studio of the second designer. "You're already dashing from one place to another with barely time to get your breath back or change clothes in between. Surely you are overstretching yourself by taking on extra clients."

I had to bite my tongue to stop myself from retorting in anger at her interference in my life. Cassie really didn't understand how my job worked. I resorted to layman's terms. "There's not so much dashing around when it comes to the shows. Although I do get a lot of work crammed into a short space of time. During any fashion week I might take pictures for a number of different clients, some in the mornings, others in the afternoon, sometimes at evening events too. That's what these two new contracts are for."

"That may be the case but from what I've seen..." Cassie shook her head, seemingly unconvinced.

"You caught me at a bad time with several extra jobs I wouldn't normally have. After I get back from Paris in early October I'll have a good long break."

"I'll hold you to that." Cassie took my arm as we crossed the busy intersection heading back to the hotel. "I still don't like the thought of you working yourself into the ground when you maybe don't need to. To me it looks like you're doing okay financially, judging by your apartment and the closet full of designer clothes."

"I am bumping along quite nicely but, like a lot of things, if you aren't in the public eye you're going to suffer and the work will dry up."

Cassie frowned. "What you're saying here is the success or failure of a business like yours hangs on your association with the big names and your visibility at events?"

"More or less, yes. Not so much the big names, although their patronage certainly helps. It's more about the perception of being part of the pack, of having a strong profile so designers recognize you and your work."

"Right." Cassie huffed loudly. "I will have to assume you know what you're doing here, and far be it for me to interfere in the smooth running of your business."

Back in the hotel room Cassie flopped down on the bed and put her hands behind her head. "What would you like to do tonight? I could try the concierge for theatre tickets or we could go out for a meal?"

I shrugged, neither of Cassie's suggestions struck a particular chord with me. "I'm easy. Why don't we stay in? Let's order something special from room service and then..."

"Now that sounds like an excellent plan." Cassie fixed me with a penetrating look. "Providing you are sure you really want to do that."

"I'm sure. We haven't had much private time on this trip and we have a long flight ahead of us tomorrow night."

"True." Cassie grinned then leapt up and shrugged out of her clothes. "I'm going to take a shower. New York always makes me feel grubby. Why don't you choose what you'd like from the room service menu and phone the order through? I'll have a steak, medium rare, with something rich and sweet to follow. Order some champagne, as well. My treat. Tell them half an hour, no more, I'm hungry."

I was hungry, too, but not for food. Seeing Cassie stride across the room, naked, set my pulse racing and my body longing for her touch. With some reluctance I curbed my desire and reached for the menu. Hopefully, my reward would come later.

Cassie emerged from the bathroom wrapped in the complimentary bath robe just as room service arrived with our meal. My grilled lemon sole with a papaya salsa was perfect and I didn't hear any complaints from Cassie who cleared her plate of steak, mushroom, tomatoes, and fries, and then polished off a large slice of chocolate gateau with cream in no time flat.

"Mmmm, that's better." Cassie sighed contentedly and topped up our glasses with the rest of the champagne. She leaned forward to peer at my dessert plate, frowning slightly. "What have you got there?"

"Key lime pie. It's good, very tangy and not too sweet."

"I've heard of key lime pie but never tasted it. May I?" Cassie picked up her fork and scooped up a small amount. "Oh, that is..." She shuddered. "...so not for me."

I laughed at the pained expression on her face. "Not such a good idea on top of that sweet chocolate cake."

"You may be right there." Cassie joined in with my laughter. Anyway... I'd better make some coffee to take the nasty taste away."

While Cassie made coffee I loaded all the dirty dishes onto the cart and then trundled it outside into the corridor ready for collection. I didn't want any interruptions to spoil what I planned to do next.

Cassie had shed the bath robe and settled herself comfortably on the bed by the time I finished pottering around. "Come and keep me company." She patted the space beside her in invitation.

"I will, very soon..." I promised before I ducked into the bathroom to freshen up. Last minute nerves almost getting the better of me. Although I'd rehearsed this in my mind the reality was still a daunting prospect but I wanted Cassie to see that I was taking our relationship seriously by doing something to demonstrate my devotion to her.

You can do this.

I took a couple of deep breaths before emerging from the bathroom, my nerves jangling. For symbolic reasons I'd chosen the same Giovanni d'Marco two piece that had featured in the disastrous first night strip.

God! My naivety and inexperience really sucked that night.

It wasn't an easy task undoing all those tiny buttons on the jacket and trying to look sexy at the same time but I did my best. Then I adopted a couple of model style poses as I discarded the jacket before I moved onto the skirt letting gravity take control until the garment pooled around my feet.

Pause. Breathe. Step out of the mess of clothes. Turn. Pose.

The litany ran through my head. I could feel Cassie's heated gaze on me, branding my skin, but I kept my own gaze lowered deferentially.

I ran my hands over my body, hoping I was doing it right, then reached around behind me to unhook my bra and let it fall away. That offered me the chance to show off my tits, the one body part of which I wasn't totally ashamed. I spent several minutes touching, tweaking, pushing and shaping until I began to get really wet. Dangerously so.

Okay, time to move on. Cassie doesn't like me to come unless she gives her consent and I don't want to incur her wrath tonight of all nights.

Concentrate!

Breaking new ground here.

I shimmied out of my panties and posed some more, showing off my cunt and my ass from every position. I knew Cassie favored certain angles and I employed all those as I carefully removed my shoes and finally my stockings.

"Come closer, honey."

Cassie's 'Mistress' voice penetrated my consciousness. I moved toward the bed keeping my gaze lowered.

"Kneel down."

I did as instructed. Totally focused on Cassie's voice, on her commands. I needed to show her I'd learnt from my previous mistakes.

"Look at me."

I obeyed. My heart jumping up and down like a jack-in-the-box.

"Thank you, honey. That was awesome." Cassie reached out and touched my lower lip then trailed her index finger down my throat and into the valley between my breasts.

"Thank you, Mistress." My throat was really tight but I managed to force the words out. "I wanted to please you."

"You did. Very much." She paused, a slight frown crossing her brow. "Would you care to please me some more?"

"Yes, Mistress." I rushed to affirm my willingness to serve her in any way she wanted.

"Fetch my bag."

I leapt up again, crossed the room to the closet, and returned with her bag. Cassie unzipped the side pocket, pulled out the two hanks of rope and a small flogger. Then she dug deeper and came up with a narrow box.

I'd seen a box like that before. The breath caught in my throat and my thoughts returned to the night Cassie had given me a collar in recognition of our mutual desire to form a D/s relationship.

"I was saving this for a special occasion," Cassie said softly. "I think that moment just arrived." She opened the box and displayed a beautiful silver collar indistinguishable from the one that Esmée and Marisa subsequently stole from me.

"It is lovely," I murmured, not knowing what else to say.

"As are you. You please me immensely." Cassie lifted the delicate object from its satin lined case and held it out to me. "Will you wear it for me as a symbol of your devotion and of your willingness to explore our relationship with an open mind?"

"Yes, Mistress, thank you. You honor me with your trust." I dropped to my knees beside the bed. "Will you put it on for me, please?" The cool metal slipped easily around my neck, the clasp settling perfectly into the hollow of my throat.

Suddenly, after weeks of suffering following that disastrous night at Out of Bounds, I felt whole again.

"I think this calls for a small celebration." Cassie leapt off the bed. "Come with me!"

I followed her across the room to where I'd left my clothes. Cassie sorted out my panties, and stockings then handed them to me. "Put these back on and I'll be right back."

Cassie was full of surprises. She returned carrying the hanks of rope and the flogger, plus a substantial flattened metal hook-like object which she fitted over the top of the bathroom door before closing it.

My mouth dried in anticipation. A hook trapped by the closed door was the perfect height to tie my wrists above my head.

Cassie arranged me against the door, feet slightly apart, taking time to get me in just the right position. "Give me your hands." She held hers together in demonstration before picking up one length of rope. With my wrists securely tied, Cassie looped the rope over the hook and tied it off on the door handle before she stood back to admire her handiwork.

I wasn't suspended, just constrained, my feet were still in contact with the floor so the strain on my arms wasn't as bad as it might otherwise have been. It felt good. Very good. Cassie picked up the flogger then paced back and forth. Sometimes touching me with the leather strands, other times standing just close enough for me to feel her breath on my face.

"You're doing really well, honey," she said quietly. "This will make it even better, I promise." She wiped the flogger over my body, teasing my tits, then up my thighs and across my sex.

The eroticism of this softly softly approach drove me wild but I knew I mustn't show any emotion or I'd incur her displeasure.

"Time to turn around." Cassie supported me as she turned my body to face the door.

Not being able to see what Cassie was doing proved even more erotic. I could only feel the sensuous kiss of leather thongs on my back and my ass, then sweeping up my legs and thighs too. The urge to stick my ass out to meet the flogger was irresistible but I soon pulled it back in when Cassie whacked me hard across the cheeks of my butt.

"Stop that." Another hard whack landed close to the first one.

"Sorry, Mistress." I screwed my eyes shut and prayed I could hold out until she granted me relief.

Thankfully, Cassie turned me around again before I disgraced myself further. She set the flogger aside, employing her mouth, tongue, and fingers to caress my body. Cassie knelt before me taking my panties and stockings down and burying her face in my sex. Her tongue probed me. Her fingers too seeking out my sensitive spots. My limbs quivered with the strain of holding back on the orgasm that was hammering at the door.

Finally, when I didn't think I could last another second, Cassie said the magic words. "Give it to me, honey. Let me have your juice. All of it." She took me with her tongue, siphoning every last drop from my cunt like it was the most precious nectar. Never had I been so grateful for the support of the rope without which I'd have surely collapsed in a heap on the floor.

Cassie untied me quickly and carried me to bed.

"You were superb, honey." She massaged my wrists and forearms slowly getting the circulation up to normal. "Let's have a quick shower and call it a night?"

I nodded. "Sounds good to me."

Back in bed, after our shower, Cassie spooned her body to mine and kissed my neck. "Goodnight, honey. I want to take you shopping tomorrow for something special before we have to leave for the airport."

Our arrival back in London early on Friday morning turned into my worst nightmare and lasted most of the day.

"Oh, my God!"

I barely registered Cassie's exclamation of horror as I stopped dead just inside the front door barely absorbing the scene of utter devastation. Somebody had wrecked my beautiful apartment smashing anything breakable and daubing bright red paint over everything else. That included the picture window upon which the intruder had left a crude message.

'FUCK YOU BITCH

THIS IS JUST FOR STARTERS'.

"Come away, honey. You can't do anything." Cassie tugged at my arm, urging me back. "You...we...can't stay here. This is now a job for the police."

I'm ashamed to say I was too numb to be of much use. I let Cassie call the police and deal with most of the questions. As to how the culprit got in the only possible explanation was that my keycard had somehow been forged, copied or skimmed. Cassie voiced her suspicion of Esmée and Marisa to the police who said they would follow up on it once the forensic examination had been completed and any other leads eliminated.

I was even too bemused to register where Cassie took me after the lengthy police interview, fingerprinting, and DNA swabs were done. Only that it was somewhere in the center of London, to an old-style apartment block in a narrow street rather than a hotel.

"Where are we?" I asked Cassie, finally emerging from my stupor to take in the apartment. It had the same look and feel as Auchtercairn, a clutter of mismatched antiques – Georgian, Victorian, even early Edwardian, nothing later, with no period particularly dominant.

Cassie shrugged and concentrated on pouring drinks into heavy cut-glass tumblers. "A family apartment." She pushed a glass of something amber into my hand. "Drink it straight down. It'll make you feel better."

Assuming it was brandy, which I sort of liked in moderation, I did as instructed and practically choked on the fiery spirit. "What on earth was that?" My head swam and I quickly handed the glass back to her for fear I would drop it.

"Single malt." Cassie's laughter lightened the mood. "A mature Talisker to be precise. What did you think of it?"

"Powerful stuff," I gasped. "Too powerful for me. I told you I wasn't into spirits."

"I know you did..." She shrugged nonchalantly. "But you were in need of something to take the edge off your shock."

"It certainly did that." I brushed the tears from my eyes and sought the nearest chair before my legs gave out. "Do you really think Esmée and Marisa were responsible for all that mess?"

"Yes, I do. Not that the police seemed keen to believe me. It might take them a while to come around to my way of thinking. In the meantime we will stay here, in hiding, until your next trip."

"You're coming to Berlin?"

"Too right I am." Cassie reached down, drew me to my feet and kissed me hard. From now on, certainly until the person responsible for this attack is safely locked up, we are joined at the hip, where you go I go too."

"Thank you." I yawned loudly.

"Come, honey." Cassie took my hand and led me down the hallway to the bedroom. "I think we both need some sleep."

Sleep, however, wasn't so easy to come by. Whilst Cassie snored quietly beside me, my brain wouldn't rest or even begin to come to terms with what had happened.

I thanked providence that I always kept my most precious work with my awards and other valuables locked away in a safety deposit box. And that most of my photographic gear was safely stored in the Tavistock Street studio. The insurance would probably cover new clothes and all the other ruined stuff.

One question remained. How could anybody have got into the apartment in the first place?

Security was pretty tight with an outer door that required a four digit pin code then the keycard for the apartment door itself.

Okay, so people regularly circumnavigated the outer door by barging in when another person was coming or going. Or getting buzzed in on the pretext of delivering a package or even a pizza. Cassie had done just that when she hunted me down. No doubt the CCTV at the entrance would give the police some clues on that score.

There were only two keycards to my door – although I assumed the building manager kept a master keycard for emergencies. I had one which was never out of my possession, and Cassie the other – the police had checked them both for clues – and we were in New York at the time of the incident so...

Oh, shit! I flung the duvet off, sweating profusely. My keycard had been out of sight on one occasion recently, in Amsterdam when I left my purse in the RV and guess who was in there all alone?

"Why so restless, honey?" Cassie roused from sleep and threw her arm across my body.

"I need to tell the police."

"Tell them what?"

"About my keycard. You remember that confrontation I had with Marisa in Amsterdam?"

"Yes?"

"I'd left my purse in the RV with all my other stuff and, when I went back after Marisa left, it had been moved. I didn't think anything of it at the time but now..."

"It may not mean—"

"Ordinarily I would agree with you but Marisa said an odd thing, 'Esmée has your card marked.' I didn't understand what she meant then but it makes a whole lot more sense now."

"Okay, honey, we'll deal with it in the morning. Now go to sleep."

"I can't... I'm too wound up by what's happened."

Cassie growled. "In that case maybe I can make you forget, for a little while at least." She rolled over and took me in her arms. Her knee spread my thighs apart as she settled her weight onto me.

She knew just the right buttons to push to get me going. Within a short while Cassie had taken me over the edge into a place where nothing mattered except the incredible high of my orgasm.

I woke next day to the reality of the situation, another police interview, plus a lack of clothes, shoes, and all the other personal items that one takes for granted. A few forays into the stores around Knightsbridge, Bond Street, and Sloane Square soon solved the clothes problem, but the rest would take a bit longer to replace.

Cassie accompanied me on a two day trip to Berlin and then back to New York for the fashion week where, to give due credit, she never left my side. I worked on autopilot with uncertainty about the future playing havoc with my nerves and, to a certain extent, to my relationship with Cassie which stagnated rather than flourished. London, Milan and Paris all passed without any incident other than a few glares from Esmée and Marisa. After a while I stopped phoning the police to check on the progress of an investigation that seemed to be going nowhere fast.

What is taking so long?

The one constant in all this trauma was Célestin. Whenever our paths crossed, her contagious enthusiasm for the upcoming trip to Auchtercairn lightened my otherwise gloomy outlook. It would be good to get to know her a little outside of work.

With the fashion circus finally behind us Cassie insisted we spend the next couple of months at Auchtercairn. Not hiding exactly, although it felt a bit like that to me, but recovering and regrouping as she termed it.

Fate, however, decreed a change of plan. A phone call from the police just twenty four hours short of our departure north put the arrangements on hold.

The following morning we presented ourselves to the police station, as instructed. Buoyed up by the summons and assuming we were to hear they'd found the culprit or made some substantial progress in the case. What we learned instead proved a devastating blow to our hopes.

Cassie was summarily arrested on suspicion of perverting the course of justice.

It appeared that the police had *undisclosed* reasons to believe that she had conspired with others to kidnap me, send those threatening notes, and cause criminal damage to my apartment in order to gain my trust for *unspecified* fraudulent purposes.

They've made a mistake.

I couldn't comprehend the enormity of these accusations even when the details were explained to me. "No! You've got it all wrong," I protested time and time again. My stomach churned and tears cascaded down my cheeks. In fact I ended up crying all the way through the extended police interview.

Cassie can't have done all this.

The denials reverberated relentlessly in my head. I didn't believe a word of the claims against her. The police, however, were adamant there was sufficient evidence to pursue this line of inquiry and they had to investigate all the facts before deciding if any charges would be laid. Even worse was to come. Cassie was granted bail while the inquiries were made but one of her bail conditions stipulated that she must not make any contact with me by phone, email, mail or in person.

"Please!" I begged the desk sergeant. "I need to speak to her, urgently, just for a couple of minutes."

"Sorry, Miss Austin, no can do." He shook his head. "You are a potential witness here. I suggest you go home and forget about her."

Some chance of that.

Totally distraught, I left the police station and wandered the streets with no idea of direction. Only later did it occur to me that I had no home to go to now. I had given up the apartment, after the attack, and never wanted to set foot in the place again.

I will never forget Cassie as long as I live.

Then it occurred to me that no matter what the police said I must return to her apartment in Curzon Street. All my stuff was there. I, at least, had the legal right to pick it up. Then I must find somewhere else to stay until this was all resolved one way or the other.

Cassie was at home. Her face so drawn she looked ten years older.

"Oh, honey..." She opened her arms and I flew into them. Our lips locked and her arms closed about me. She finally broke the kiss."Where have you been all afternoon?"

"Walking. Trying to make sense of this mess." I shrugged. "Why did it happen?"

"I don't know, honey." She stroked my cheek. "I was so worried about you."

"There was no need." My tears overflowed once again. "Who did this to you...to us?" Stupid question. I knew the answer, deep down, even before the words left my mouth.

Cassie confirmed my thoughts. "Esmée has exacted her revenge. This is the culmination of everything that has happened before. Her final throw of the dice."

"How can she hope to get away with such lies?"

"She won't, but it will take time – probably months – to resolve. She no doubt hopes that the waiting, or the uncertainty, will destroy us." Cassie held me from her, a frown creasing her brow. "We must be very careful, honey. You never know who is watching, or looking for evidence to make further accusations against me. Do you understand the implications if I'm caught with you?"

"Not exactly... What can they do to us?"

"To me, honey. Just me. You're not under any restrictions but I could have my bail revoked and end up behind bars for the duration."

"But you haven't done anything wrong," I protested, my voice cracking up. "I thought this country prided itself on a premise of innocent until proven guilty? This situation rather smacks of guilty until proven innocent."

"The police need to work that out for themselves and until they do I'm stuck in this limbo. Come..." Cassie led me into the bedroom. "I can't let you go without showing you how much I care."

The feeling was mutual. We fell onto the bed, tearing at clothes as if in a race to see who could get naked first. Our lovemaking was urgent and deeply satisfying.

Cassie kissed me, silencing my post orgasmic gasps, her breathing as ragged as mine "You can't stay here any longer, honey, that's for sure. Much as I want you to it's impossible."

'I know..." I tried to hold myself together for her sake. "I wish I could be here to help and give you strength but..."

"You must go to Auchtercairn. Hamish and Effie will look after you and keep you safe until this nightmare is over."

"No, I don't want to go up there without you." I snuggled closer.

"You can't stay in London, it'll be too risky. Besides which, I couldn't bear the thought of you being so close yet not having you in my bed.

"I'll go to Cornwall. That's far enough away from London and I know of a quiet place on the Falmouth estuary where I can hide while you get this problem sorted out.

Cassie shook her head. I'd rather you went to Scotland, but if you're sure Esmée won't find you there... Will you drive?"

"No, I'll go down by train and leave Jazzy in London, she's safely locked up in the garage. If I need transport I'll hire something untraceable for as long as I need it. St Anthony is really quiet, very peaceful and remote. I stayed there, as a child, long before Esmée. I shall be perfectly safe."

"Okay, but keep in touch. I know we're not supposed to communicate but I can't bear the thought of you out there all on your own. Anything could happen to you."

"Don't be silly." I kissed her softly. "I'm a big girl and I did okay before you came into my life."

"I know, honey, but Esmée may be looking for a way to get at you now that I'm effectively out of the picture."

"She'll have a hard job in a place like St Anthony."

Cassie grunted. "While I think of it, you'd better not send any postcards or letters, they'll be too easy to intercept, and the same applies to phone calls. I'll get a cheap used notepad from the market tomorrow, something with wifi that I can use anywhere, and set up an anonymous email address for Piper and you should do the same for Tavish. I'll find a way to send a text to your cell with the details of the account." She grinned. "Nobody is going to worry about two horses emailing each other."

"Okay." I shook my head, smiling at her inventiveness. "And before it gets forgotten, one of us will need to tell Célestin that her visit is off. Shall I do that?"

"If you would, honey." Cassie stroked my arm. "You know her better than I do. I'll leave it to you to decide how much to tell her."

We showered together, savoring every moment of the precious time left to us then I dressed and got online to book a hotel near Paddington from where I could catch a train to the Westcountry the following day. I left calling a cab until last; it seemed so final.

My bags were already packed from our previously scheduled departure. I added my cosmetics and washing bag, kissed Cassie one last time and forced myself to walk out the door. I knew if I looked back I would never have the strength to leave.

Tears misted my vision all the way to the hotel and for a good part of the train ride. The further away I got from Cassie the greater the pain of our separation. I broke my trip in Exeter, to stay a few nights in a comfortable hotel close to the cathedral. It gave me the opportunity to make the necessary arrangements for accommodation, buy a few clothes and shoes, things more suitable for the country, plus a new tablet with wifi for portable use. I hoped there would be a good signal for my cell phone in St, Anthony, and a fast internet connection for my laptop too, but I needed to be prepared for any eventuality. In a worst case scenario I could always catch the ferry over to St. Mawes or Falmouth for supplies and hook up to a free wifi connection.

Célestin was appalled when I called her with the news of Cassie's arrest. "You must come to me in Paris," she offered without hesitation. "Esmée and Marisa will not be able to find you here."

I declined her invitation, explaining that I wanted to be on hand if anything happened. Although my excuse was somewhat lame since I could have got to London from Paris by Eurostar much faster than by train or plane from Cornwall but I doubt Célestin realized that. I put on a brave face and told her, "You must come to Auchtercairn next year once this business is behind us."

"I'll look forward to it, chérie," Célestin said. "Please keep me informed of any developments and stay strong. Justice will prevail."

By the end of the week I was settled into a cozy cottage just a few steps from the St. Mawes ferry. A tiny walled garden surrounding the cottage gave me an extra feeling of security. Walking on the traffic free peninsular was a real pleasure after London and all the busy cities I'd visited over the past months. The only thing missing was Cassie. How I wished I could share this with her.

We'd made contact, via our equine identities, whilst I was staying in Exeter and found exchanging emails easy. We even tried a couple of IM sessions but sadly Skype defeated us.

I filled my days with planning my work schedule for the coming season, and exploring the locality with my camera. Landscape photography wasn't really my thing but it kept me from brooding and I amassed enough material to consider publishing a photo-journal of my sojourn when this was all over.

A month into my exile Cassie booked into a hotel for the afternoon – she was on a nightly curfew from 6pm to 6am so overnight was out – during which time we jointly spent a small fortune having phone sex.

Cassie phoned me to begin the foreplay. "Please tell me that you're wearing your sexy lingerie." It was clear from Cassie's voice that she expected, no demanded, an affirmative.

"Sorry to disappoint but I've been out all morning taking pictures and I'm still wearing jeans and a sweatshirt. Give me five minutes to change and I'll call you back."

"Don't keep me waiting honey..." She gave me her room number and hung up.

I phoned her back, right on time although slightly out of breath from rushing, and put the phone on speaker.

"Okay, honey... Cassie's 'Mistress' voice oozed silk. I want you to strip for me. You know the routine. I want to picture you strutting your stuff."

She doesn't want much.

I'd stripped for her a number of times now but still found doing so a bit of a challenge. Although maybe it wouldn't be so hard this time with just me, the cell phone, and the mirror.

"Think back to New York," I said, attempting to ramp up the tension straight away. "I'm watching myself in the full length mirror so I can see what you saw then. I've unbuttoned the jacket and it's hanging open. I can see my bra... and my tits..." I smiled.

This half undressed view is kind of sexy.

"Okay, honey...I get the picture. Keep talking."

"Now I'm removing the jacket, just shrugging out of very slowly and letting it slide down my arms. It's off, and I'm using my hands to push my tits up. They're aching for freedom but I'm going to take this really slowly."

"Imagine those are my hands, honey. Tell me how it feels to have my fingers spanning the full weight of those gorgeous tits and my thumbs circling your nipples through the lace."

"Oh...that is so good." I copied her description to the letter. "My nipples are really hard."

"Good...now I want you to pull the bra down and lift your tits out. No, don't undo the clasp."

I did as she instructed, forcing myself to savor the moment. A spike of awareness contracted my insides and I bit my lip to stifle the gasp of pleasure.

"They're out," I confirmed. Admiring the result in the mirror. Being forced up like this my nipples were darker and extra prominent, begging for attention.

Dare I risk a quick flick or pull?

"Leave your tits alone!" The injunction scythed through the air like the crack of a whip.

How did Cassie read my mind?

I resisted the urge to disobey.

"Yes, Mistress."

"Now lose the skirt."

This departure from the norm caught me unawares. I forced a sharp hiss of breath through clenched teeth and focused on her instructions. Once I ran the zipper down, the skirt needed no help to slither down my thighs to the floor.

"Okay, the skirt is off." I waited anxiously for her next instruction.

"Have you got the toy bag handy?"

Yes, Mistress." She had mailed me a package of toys in advance and I had the bag hanging on the door handle.

"Good... Now step out of the clothes and stand up against the wall with your feet a little apart. Tell me what you see in the mirror."

I rushed to do as requested, backing up against the wall close by the bedroom door, and staring at my reflection in the mirror. I shook my head.

"I look like a tart, a slut – a whore even – standing here with my hair all messed up, and my tits hanging out, not to mention the black underwear and stockings."

Cassie was fond of making me take up this pose, she liked to tie my hands above my head and tease me with a flogger, holding me on the brink of a climax for ages before letting me come. That was out of the question here, but no doubt she had something else in mind.

"That's right, you're my personal little whore." Cassie's voice issued softly from the phone. "Get the nipple clamps from the bag and put them on. Tell me when you're done."

The initial stab of pain from the clamps forced me to regulate my breathing. Then the tug of the chain sent waves of gut-clenching fire to my cunt. Oh, mercy me, I was already dripping wet, it would take no more than the smallest stimulation to tip me over the edge into free fall.

"They're on now."

"Excellent. You're doing really well, honey. Now find the pink dildo and switch it to slow."

I heard Cassie take a deep breath.

"Are you ready?

"I'm ready, Mistress," I confirmed, my voice a trifle unsteady.

"I want you to tease yourself with the dildo, don't be shy, wipe it over your crotch but keep away from your clit. No cheating."

The first swipe replenished the fire in my loins, the second fueled a sharp intake of breath, and the third nearly destroyed me. I widened my stance, dragging the fingernails of my free hand over the wall.

"Please let me come." My plea turned into a moan.

"That sounds perfect. You are doing really well," Cassie praised me, her voice hushed. "Just a little while longer, honey. You know you want to hold on to please me."

Yes, I did. Pleasing Cassie gave me an incredible high. I couldn't describe it and I was too far gone to try. I just listened to her voice and gritted my teeth waiting for her to release me from the torment and transport me to the place she had created especially for me.

"Please, Mistress..."

"One more time...then I want you to drive that dildo deep inside you. Imagine it's my hand, I have you trapped against the wall. Can you feel me fucking you hard with my fingers?"

"I can, Mistress. Please..." I begged her. My legs were trembling so much from holding back I feared they would give out on me before Cassie said the magic words.

"Okay, honey. Let it all out. Just for me. I want to hear you come."

I have no idea what I said or did once the orgasm gripped me and swept everything from my mind. My next conscious moment found me on the floor in a heap sobbing uncontrollably. A nice sobbing I must add. Totally drained but at peace with myself.

"That was beautiful, honey. So beautiful." Cassie's voice was soft and calming. "You are very special to me."

"And you to me." I hiccupped. "Will you let me give you something in return?"

"I'm good, honey," Cassie's 'Mistress' voice returned warning me not to argue. "This was never about me. I must go now. We'll do this again next month. Bye, honey."

"Don't go," I begged her but the line was dead. Devastation hit me in the guts. I swore. I cried. I screamed. I threw things. And above all I ranted at the authorities for putting us through this torment for no good reason. Couldn't they see that Esmée was manipulating them, just as she'd manipulated me for all those years?

Another month passed and another. We never repeated the phone sex, it was too traumatic. A miserable Christmas came and went. Then suddenly on the second Monday in January, just as I'd began cancelling my commitments citing ill health, it was all over. Cassie was freed from her bail, at the same time Esmée and Marisa were arrested, charged, and remanded in custody.

I caught the first available train to London and found Cassie waiting for me on the platform at Paddington station. I flew into her arms totally oblivious to all the hustle and bustle of the station platform.

Sadly, I have no words to describe the intense emotions of this moment. I just knew I never wanted to be parted from her ever again.

We arrived in Scotland late on Thursday afternoon.

My feelings were mixed when I drove Jazzy into the same yard from where I'd fled at the crack of dawn some twelve months previously. Now, with everything that had happened in between that previous visit seemed like a different era.

Cassie was out of the vehicle almost before I braked to a halt, rushing to pet the same bevy of barking, tail wagging, dogs that had greeted us before.

Later, we dined in style, off fine china, sitting side by side at one end of a massive oak table that could have seated more than thirty guests. Effie, Hamish's wife, bustled around setting the food out on a sideboard so we could help ourselves having insisted we use the grand dining hall rather than the kitchen. "It's so good to have you home again, Miss Cassie," she said. Effie had done us proud, producing an excellent feast: clear soup, followed by leg of lamb with a redcurrant glaze, then individual open apple tarts served with thick cream and a raspberry coulis. All local ingredients she assured us, smiling broadly.

After dinner Cassie gave me a guided tour of the castle, something that she'd omitted on my last visit. Let's face it we had other things on our minds that night. She held my hand and gave me a potted history of each area as we sauntered from room to room often stopping to kiss and cuddle as the mood took us. We had a lot of time to make up.

A lot of the original fortification had been destroyed during the seventeen forty five rebellion but subsequent generations had repaired the remains and added their own stamp to the fabric. She left the dungeon to last. The tower, in which it was situated, was the oldest part of the castle built in the early sixteen hundreds to hold a commanding position at the entrance to a narrow sea loch.

In the light from electric candles that flickered almost as eerily as the real thing, my gaze took in the array of restraints which hung from the walls, each separated by filmy, red-silk drapes. The spanking stool and swing still stood ready for use in the middle of the room. My gaze traveled on to the St. Andrews Cross set into an alcove to one side, and, the pièce de résistance, a black wrought-iron, four-poster bed dressed in red and black silk.

Nothing much had changed.

And finally I turned to the table seeking the red spaghetti string flogger that Cassie had used on me to great effect. My skin prickled, growing goose bumps with the memory. I wanted to recreate that special moment without delay.

We'd celebrated our reunion in London, a couple of days after Cassie was officially released from her bail conditions. Then again in a motel room on the drive up to Scotland. Even symbolically in a pull off at the very top of the Drumochter Pass, by the sign that read *'Fàilte don Ghàidhealtachd'* Welcome to the Highlands. However, here in this place where it all began, I knew our coming together would be something special.

Finally, Cassie drew me close. "It's late, honey, we have an eternity to play here together. I'd rather like to unwind from the long drive and get some sleep before we embark on anything too ambitious. I promise you tomorrow and every day after that I will honor your devotion, your love, and your commitment to me."

About The Author

Dalia Craig loves to both read and write a variety of contemporary erotic fiction. While her particular leaning is towards lesbian romance, her writing encompasses all heat levels and diverse genre. She has a number of eBooks to her credit and is also a contributor to several print anthologies including: Where the Girls Are: Urban Lesbian Erotica, Best Lesbian Romance 2010 both from Cleis Press. Plus the Goldie 2013 nominated anthology, Sapphic Planet.

Bound by Consent, her first print novella, was launched at the GCLS event during Women's Week 2012.

You can connect with her online at:
www.daliacraig.com

Other Titles By Dalia Craig

Full Circle
Meeting of Minds
Night Games
Slave to Lust
Seduced by a Stranger
Consuming Passion
Desire And Deception
A Reckless Affair
Weathering The Storm,
Loving Ellie,
Taming Bryana
Hold Me Tight
All For Love

Lydian Press is dedicated to bringing you the finest
GLBTQ erotic literature on the web.

Visit us on the web at:
http://lydianpress.com

www.ingramcontent.com/pod-product-compliance
Lightning Source LLC
Chambersburg PA
CBHW051105050726
47592CB00002B/685